The Bridges in Paris

Michele Sobel Spirn

FOUR CORNERS PUBLISHING CO.

NEW YORK

Four Corners Publishing Company
45 West 10th Street, Suite 4J, New York, NY 10011

Printed in U.S.A.

Cover illustration by Catherine Huerta
Maps by Jay Karamales, Olórin Press

03 04 02 01 00   5 4 3 2 1

Library of Congress Cataloging-in-Publication Data

Spirn, Michele.
      The Bridges in Paris / Michele Sobel Spirn.
      p. cm. -- (Going to series)
      Summary: While their parents are at a conference, sisters Robin and
      Jo are left to see the sights of Paris in the care of a secretive woman
      and the girls find themselves involved in a sequence of mysterious
      events.
      ISBN 1-893577-04-X
      [1. Sisters--Fiction. 2. Paris (France)--Fiction. 3. France--Fiction.
      4. Mystery and detective stories.] I. Title. II. Series

      PZ7.S757 Br 2000
      [Fic]--dc21   00-059325

For Steve and Josh,
and the last time we saw Paris,
and for Danièle Gobillon,
thanks for the radish man
and all your help.

CONTENTS

CHAPTER ONE

Go Away

"I can't believe we're leaving you girls in Paris," said Mrs. Bridge, pushing back her thick red hair.

"It's not as if we're abandoning them," Mr. Bridge said. "We'll be back in two weeks, after our conferences in the south of France are over. We agreed that Paris would be the best place to meet afterwards, and I'm sure the girls will enjoy staying here."

"But we just got here and I can't help worrying. We don't know very much about Mme Georges, even though Aunt Mary's friend's daughter stayed with her last year. Maybe the girls should come with us," said Mrs. Bridge.

"What would we do at a conference on dead writers?" asked Robin Bridge. "Or one on library science. Really!" She looked at her twelve-year-old sister, Jo, who was hopping from one foot to another. "I'm fourteen. I won't get into any trouble."

"And neither will I," said Jo. "After all, we'll be with a bunch of kids and Mme Georges. I hope it will be fun."

"Aunt Mary said her friend's daughter had a good time at Mme Georges's and Elise Nicholson raved about it," said their mother. "I want you to take advantage of Paris with all its culture. The Louvre!

1

The Musée D'Orsay! So much to see! Maybe you'll even learn a little French. I'm sorry you both chose to take Spanish instead."

"Yes, Mom," said Robin, but her thoughts leaned more towards seeing some French department stores and shopping for new clothes to show off back home in New Jersey.

"Maybe there'll be a mystery for us to solve like we did in London," said Jo, her brown eyes lighting up at the thought. Two weeks before, when the family was in London, Robin had gotten the wrong suitcase by mistake at the airport, and the girls had had many adventures as a result.

"No mysteries," said their father firmly. He looked around at the huge Gare du Nord, one of Paris's several major railway stations, and the bustle of people hurrying under its high glass ceiling. "There'll be plenty to see in Paris."

Jo sniffed the warm summer air. "And smell. Why does Paris smell so funny?"

"That's the smell of cigarettes and coffee," said Mrs. Bridge. She looked at her watch. "Mme Georges should be here by now. Our train leaves soon. I hope we don't miss it."

Robin glanced at the crowds of people dragging suitcases and rushing up the escalators to find their trains. She was particularly struck by a woman dressed in a black suit. The woman had a streak of white running through her dark hair and wore a thick gold necklace and earrings.

"I bet that's Mme Georges," Robin thought to herself. The woman seemed to be coming their way.

"Ah, M. Bridge, Mme Bridge," a high voice behind Robin said. "I am Mme Amélie Georges."

Robin turned to see a tall, thin woman dressed in tan pants and a tan shirt greeting her parents. The woman tossed back her dark blonde hair and extended her hand to Mr. Bridge.

"And this must be Robin and Jo," she said. Robin stared at her, fascinated. While not as distinguished looking as the woman with the white streak in her hair, Mme Georges was definitely good looking. Her hair was straight and shiny and cut one side longer than the other in a style Robin had never seen. She wore a white sweater tossed over her shoulders and a large diamond ring twinkled on her finger. On her feet were open-toed brown shoes with the highest heels Robin had ever seen.

"Your girls are charming," said Mme Georges to Mr. and Mrs. Bridge. "I am sure we will have such a good time together."

"Are there lots of other kids?" Jo asked.

"Not so many now in July. There is my niece Sylvie, and Mario, you will enjoy him, he is so *amusant*—ah, how you say?—funny, and then there is Marc, you will like him. *Oui*, and Sophie."

"And I'm sure the girls will see lots of educational sights," said Mr. Bridge.

"But of course," said Mme Georges, "we are in Paris. *Par example*, tomorrow we will see something exciting, La Course des Garçons de Café."

"What is that?" asked Mrs. Bridge.

"It's the race of the *garçons*, uh, waiters. Every year they race carrying trays that are filled with glasses and plates. The real race is held in June, but this year there is a special race for charity in July. It is very amusing to see."

Mrs. Bridge looked doubtful, and Mr. Bridge shook his head.

"Ah, but after that, we go to the Musée D'Orsay," said Mme Georges. "And of course there is the Louvre. We try to show the children the real Paris."

Mr. Bridge looked as if he were about to say something, when Mrs. Bridge gave a small shriek. "Our train—there up on the display board. I don't know—girls . . ."

"Mom, we'll be fine," said Robin firmly.

Mme Georges tactfully turned away as Robin and Jo hugged their parents and said good-bye.

"Remember, you can always call us in Cannes," Mrs. Bridge said. "You've got the phone number of the hotel and the address."

"Everything will be fine, Mom," said Robin. "You got pictures of the place we're staying, you got recommendations, everybody who stayed with Mme Georges thought it was cool. Stop worrying!"

She grabbed her sister's hand and they began dragging their suitcases across the crowded floor of the train station.

"This way, *mes petites,*" said Mme Georges. She took them out a side door and into a line of people waiting for taxis.

"I thought France would look different," said Jo, "but everyone looks normal."

"Yes, that is a lesson of travel," said Mme Georges. "People are people wherever one goes."

With that, she opened the door of a small white cab and motioned to the girls to get inside. The taxi driver put their suitcases in the trunk and they sped off.

Honk, honk! Honk, honk!

"What's that noise?" asked Robin.

"*Les gendarmes.* The police," Mme Georges replied. She seemed lost in thought as they raced past old stone buildings and cafés where people lounged outside in the hot July sunshine, drinking coffee at tiny tables.

Finally, the cab pulled up at a small, white building on a quiet side street.

"And here we are!" said Mme Georges.

Inside, the house was cool and dark. Mme Georges rang a small bell she picked up from a little table.

"Nicolette!" she called.

"*Je viens! Je viens!*"

"She is coming," Mme Georges said to the girls.

A plump woman dressed in black with a white apron tied around her waist struggled up a back staircase.

While Mme Georges explained who the girls were to Nicolette, Robin and Jo looked around. The hall they were in led to a small room with several chairs and a big, red sofa. A TV stood in the corner across from a big fireplace.

"I am sorry," said Mme Georges. "The others are out now. But Nicolette will show you to your room and you can wash up for dinner. Tonight, we go to a very famous restaurant, Le Procope. It is the oldest restaurant in Paris."

"What will we eat?" asked Jo. "Do they have pizza?"

Mme Georges laughed. "Pizza! Absolutely not! You are in Paris, you must eat like Parisians. Perhaps onion soup, perhaps snails."

"Snails!" Jo shrieked.

"Mme Georges is just teasing, aren't you?" asked Robin.

"A little. But we do eat snails. They are very good with butter and garlic."

Jo still looked horrified as the girls climbed the stairs to their room. Nicolette opened the door, showed them where the bathroom was down the hall, and gave them each a key to their room.

The girls looked around the bedroom. There were white curtains that billowed out against pink wallpaper. A small white desk and chair and two wooden dressers rested on deep pink carpeting.

"This is better than London," said Jo. "But we still have to run down the hall to the bathroom."

"At least I know how to use the shower now," said Robin. Her struggles with the handheld shower in London had soaked her and the bathroom.

As the girls unpacked, they talked about what they wanted to do in Paris.

"I'd like to shop," said Robin. "Do you think we'll get the chance?"

"I don't know," said Jo. "I'm not sure how strict Mme Georges is going to be."

"She doesn't look very strict," said Robin. "Maybe she'll give us some time off on our own."

"That'd be great," said Jo. "I want to do something fun. I don't want to spend my time in boring old museums."

"We promised Mom and Dad we'd go to the Louvre," said Robin.

"Oh, yeah," said Jo, "but they can't expect us to spend all our time in museums. And after all, they're not here, so we can have some say in how we spend our time."

"I don't know about that," Robin said.

"We'd better get ready for dinner. It's six-thirty," said Jo.

"What do you think the other kids will be like?" asked Robin.

"Let's go and find out," said Jo. "They must be back by now."

The girls washed and changed, and then walked down the steep stairs to the main hall. Voices and laughter drifted towards them from the room with the fireplace.

Robin and Jo peeked in. A small blonde girl was seated in front of the TV, laughing at a cartoon show. A dark-haired boy lounged on the red sofa, reading a book, while a girl with glasses and brown hair played checkers with an older boy with blond hair.

"Hello," said Robin, shyly.

Jo bounced into the room. "Hi, I'm Jo. Who are you?"

"Hello, Jo," said the girl with brown hair and glasses. "My aunt said you and your sister were coming today. I'm Sylvie."

"Oh, I guess you're Mme Georges's niece," said Robin.

"Yes, I help my aunt out from time to time, like now. I should be studying but my aunt needs me."

"Let me introduce you," she said. "This boy is Mario. He's from Italy." She pointed to the dark-haired boy reading the book. "Mario, this is Robin and Jo."

"*Enchanté.*" Mario put his finger in the book to mark his place and smiled at the girls.

"*Parlez-vous français?*" he asked.

"No, they don't speak French," said Sylvie. "Mario speaks no English," she said to the girls.

Robin thought of mentioning the little French-English dictionary she had brought with her, but decided not to.

"This angel is Sophie," said Sylvie, indicating the small blonde girl. "She is the youngest here. Her parents are in Egypt on business, and she is staying with us for a week."

The little girl smiled at them and then turned back to her TV show.

"And I am Marc," said the blond boy. "I work part-time here and go to school in Paris during the year."

"Are you in high school?" Robin asked.

"No, I am in my first year at university," Marc said.

"I'll be going into my first year in high school," said Robin. "I'm fourteen."

"I am eighteen, Marc is nineteen, and Mario is fifteen. Sophie is ten," said Sylvie.

"Ready for dinner?" Mme Georges swept in. She had changed into a black dress, pearls, and black open-toed shoes with huge heels. "We can walk. It's just across the way here."

She led the group out of the house, up the block, across the Boulevard St. Germain, and down a narrow side street.

Robin looked at the little storefronts as they passed. Waiters beckoned from restaurants draped in red awnings. Couples sipped coffee and smoked cigarettes at little tables in front of cafés. A rich, buttery smell came from a bakery. When Robin looked in the window, she saw sugared pastries and fruit tarts as well as marzipan animals parading across the shelves.

"*Voilà!*" Mme Georges stopped in front of a small restaurant and ushered them in. Inside the place was dark and quiet. The walls were painted a brownish red and a red velvet curtain hung from one wall.

A stout woman dressed in black showed them to their table and called, "Jules! Jules!"

Robin sat down between Jo and Marc. Sylvie sat across from them, next to Mario and Sophie. Mme Georges arranged herself at the head of the table.

A waiter came scurrying up and stopped short when he saw Mme Georges. Robin could see his face turn pale.

"*Bon soir,*" he said.

"That means 'good evening,'" said Marc to Robin.

"Well, let us order," said Mme Georges to her group. "I think *steak frites* for everyone, yes?"

"That's not some kind of snails, is it?" asked Jo, wrinkling her nose.

"No, no, calm yourself," said Mme Georges. "It is steak with fries. You have that in the U.S., don't you?"

Jo heaved a sigh. "Of course," she said.

The waiter smiled sympathetically at Jo and took the order. He then leaned over to Mme Georges and said something quietly. Robin heard it, but pretended not to notice.

As he served them crusty bread, and then the hot steak and crisp golden fries, his hands shook. Robin smiled at him reassuringly, and he smiled faintly back.

But after she had finished eating, when he whisked the thick white plate away, his hands trembled so the plate crashed to the floor.

"*Pardon,*" the waiter murmured.

"Do you have such bad waiters in America?" Mme Georges asked, sneering.

"Anyone can make a mistake," Robin said, instantly feeling sorry for the waiter. He glanced up at her while the stout woman scolded him, saying loudly in English for their benefit, "You must be more careful, Jules. Tourists do not like clumsy waiters."

Marc, who sat next to Robin, paid no attention, keeping up a steady stream of chatter. He told Robin about the terrible tests he had had to take to get into the university, and how he had had to devote every day of an entire year to studying for them.

"Is it like that in the U.S.?" he asked.

"Not really," Robin said. "There are tests we take to get into college, but we don't spend a year studying for them."

As they left the restaurant, Robin said, "I forgot something." She ran back to Jules, who was standing by the door, and said, "Don't worry. I know you weren't clumsy. I drop things all the time."

Jules smiled at her and bowed. Then Robin ran back to the group. Strolling back to the house, Marc continued to discuss the differences between French and American schools, while Jo ran on ahead with Sophie.

"But perhaps it is worth it to study the way we do—"

"Excuse me," Robin broke in, a bit desperately. "But I heard a French expression today. What does '*va t'en*' mean?"

"It is a not very polite way of saying 'go away,'" said Marc. "Did someone say that to you?"

"Oh, no," said Robin. She didn't tell him the waiter had said it to Mme Georges.

"I won't tell Marc the other French word I heard the waiter say," Robin thought to herself. She didn't need a translation for that one. It was much the same in English: "*dangereux*" or "dangerous."

Do Not Tell

That night Robin tossed and turned, trying not to worry about what she had heard.

"Probably I didn't hear it right," she thought, as she pounded her pillow. She was glad Jo was such a heavy sleeper.

Finally, she managed to fall asleep. She was still sleeping soundly when a loud knock on the door made her sit up in bed suddenly.

"*Bonjour!*" And then a long string of French she didn't understand.

"I guess it's time to get up. Come on, Jo, time to get dressed."

Jo opened one eye, looked at Robin, and rolled over again.

"Come on, otherwise we'll miss breakfast," Robin said.

"Do you think they serve snails for breakfast?" Jo asked fearfully.

But when they went downstairs, Nicolette served them steaming cups of hot chocolate and flaky rolls called croissants. As Jo spread hers with butter and jam, Robin asked, "What time do we leave for the waiters' race?"

"Right after breakfast," Sylvie said.

"Can we walk?" asked Jo.

"No, we'll take the métro. It's faster," said Mme Georges.

When they got off the train, Jo was entranced with the map in the métro.

"Look, you push where you want to go and it lights up!" she cried. She pointed to where a string of lights showed the route.

"Come on, Jo," said Sylvie. "We don't want to be late."

They hurried up the stairs and into a huge crowd. Jo wriggled her way to the front, dragging Robin. Robin was so entranced by the building in front of which the waiters were gathering that she forgot to look at the racers.

"This is our city hall, the Hôtel de Ville" said Marc, who had followed them. "You see what is written in the middle there—that means 'liberty, equality, fraternity'—that is the motto of the French Revolution."

Robin stared at the huge building made of gray-white stone with seven gray roofs. At the top were winged statues with women's faces. Below those, statues decorated the entire building. Two big, black, wrought iron doors with gold trim guarded the entrances.

Robin realized that Jo was still with her at the front of the crowd, but Marc had dropped back and she didn't know where Mme Georges and the rest were. Even if she wanted to look for them, the crowd held her and Jo firmly in place.

Now Robin became aware of the waiters lining up on the broad plaza. They wore black vests and white aprons.

"Look!" cried Jo. "There's Jules. Hi, Jules."

He glanced over and saw them, and looked at the crowd carefully. Then he came over to them.

"Hi, Jules," Jo said. "Good luck."

"I must to leave something with you. So I can make the race, please?" he asked. Out of his pocket, he took a small package. "Do not tell a one," he said.

Robin took the package. "We won't tell anyone," she said. "I'll put it in my backpack," said Jo. "It'll be safe there." She opened the zipper and tucked the package inside the black sack.

Jules looked around and then put his finger to his lips.

"Promise. Do not tell. I will return after the race. You meet me here. And take care. What you have, it is important."

Then he slipped back into the crowd of waiters lined up on the plaza.

Bong! Bong! The bells of the clock in the center of the building began to sound the hour. When the last bell had rung, Robin heard a shot from a starter pistol. The waiters raced off, carrying their precious cargo of glasses, wine, and trays.

The crowd started to melt away, many spectators wandering off to the nearby cafés.

"That was very amusing, wasn't it?" asked Mme Georges, who suddenly appeared beside them.

"I enjoyed it," said Robin, "but the building is really special."

"Yes," said Mme Georges, absently. "Was that Jules I saw talking to you?"

"No," said Robin. "It was another waiter. He dropped something and Jo gave it back to him."

"I see," said Mme Georges. "Well, we can have a soft drink and then come back for the end of the race."

As the girls crossed the street behind Mme Georges, Jo said to Robin, "That was quick thinking."

"He told us not to tell anyone," said Robin.

"Do you think he meant Mme Georges?" Jo asked.

"I don't know, but I don't think we should take any chances," said Robin.

"This is spooky," said Jo, shivering. "It's like those mysteries you're always reading."

"He'll be back after the race, and then the whole thing will be cleared up," Robin said.

But after the winner was congratulated at the end of the race, Jules didn't turn up.

"He said he'd meet us right here," Jo said.

"Girls, we're ready to leave," Mme Georges said.

"Can we stay a little longer?" Robin asked. "I'd really like to study the building."

"How will you get back to the house for lunch?" Mme Georges replied.

"I'll stay with them, Aunt Amélie," said Sylvie.

"Very well," said Mme Georges, "but don't be too late. We want to go to the Musée D'Orsay this afternoon."

"You will love the Musée D'Orsay," Sylvie said. "Everyone does. But perhaps you will tell me a bit about New York? You must know it well living so close to it."

She leaned forward and her green eyes snapped behind her glasses.

"I'll tell you," Robin said. She started talking to Sylvie about Central Park and Fifth Avenue, all the while leading her to the other side of the building.

"And the clothes! Do women really wear tattoos in New York?"

Sylvie questioned Robin, as she walked with the older girl. The sun dipped behind the clouds. As Sylvie chattered away, a man in a black vest and white apron walked towards Robin. She was just about to greet him when she saw it wasn't Jules.

"Papa!" Children rushed to his side, and she saw him kiss them and swing them around.

Where was Jules? Robin was impatient. They must have missed him somehow.

She and Sylvie strolled back from the other side of the building.

"Anything?" Robin whispered to Jo.

Jo shook her head.

The three girls rode back on the métro, Robin and Jo puzzling over their mystery, Sylvie lost in thought over what Robin had told her about New York.

After lunch, Mme Georges suggested a brief rest for everyone. Jo and Robin ran up to their room. Jo took the package out of her backpack.

"What do you think we should do with this?" Jo asked.

"I've got an idea," Robin said. "Let's take it to the restaurant tonight. Jules is sure to be there. We can give it to him then."

"Excellent," said Jo. "But will we be able to go there by ourselves? Mme Georges is worse than Mom and Dad. We haven't been able to go off alone since we got here."

"Surely she'd let us walk across the street alone. After all, we're not babies," said Robin.

"I don't know," said Jo. "We'd better have a backup plan in case she doesn't let us go out alone."

"How about if we ask to go back to Le Procope? We'll say it was so delicious we want to go again," said Robin.

"Good idea," said Jo. "Actually, it wasn't bad."

That afternoon, the group trekked to the Musée D'Orsay. Robin had to agree with Sylvie, it was fascinating.

"It is an old train station that was saved and turned into a museum," Marc told her.

Inside, the long halls of the train station had been transformed into galleries, each one displaying paintings by a different group of artists. Marc took Robin up to the Impressionist gallery, where she saw misty paintings by Claude Monet.

"These are my favorites," she said, "particularly the one of the cathedral."

Jo bounded into the gallery.

"Did you see the big clock?" she asked. She grabbed Robin's hand and dragged her to see the old-fashioned clock smack in the middle of a restaurant in the museum.

"Marc told me that the one thing they made sure to save from the train station was the clock," Jo said.

When they left the museum, they walked slowly along a long stretch of gray stone wall over which Robin and Jo could peer at the Seine River. On some sections of the wall there were what looked like dark green cupboards. Some of the cupboards were open and men displayed post cards, prints, drawings, and cartoons in them.

"Look! There's a copy of a Monet," said Robin.

"Yes," said Marc. "It looks good and it's cheap, too. Only twenty-five francs."

"I'll buy it," said Robin. The man took the little print and rolled it up with tissue paper.

"*Mademoiselle*," he said and handed it to her.

"I'll put it up in my room at home," said Robin. "It'll remind me of Paris."

"Do you like Paris?" Marc asked.

"It's so beautiful," Robin said. "How could anyone not like it?"

"It is beautiful, but hard," said Sylvie, joining them. "It is not easy living here. Sometimes, I think I must get away."

"Don't you like it?" Robin asked.

"I can't explain. Too hard in English," she said, and she walked on quickly.

"Sylvie has perhaps what you call the difficult life," said Marc. "Her aunt is not an easy woman to live with."

"I see," said Robin. She didn't know what else to say so she changed the subject.

The light flickered on the water, and Robin watched the boats go by.

"I'd like to be on one of those," she said.

"Oh, we'll probably do that," said Marc. "We usually go on a boat at night. Paris looks its best then."

"Have you always lived here?" Robin asked.

"Oh, no," Marc said. "I live outside of Paris—in the suburbs, you'd call it. I am here because it's too far to go back and forth from the university."

"Don't your parents miss you?" Robin asked.

"There are eight of us," he said, with a little smile. "My parents are glad I can get a good start. They're happy I'm here."

"Do you go home much?" Robin asked.

"Now and then," Marc said. "But Paris is my home now."

"*Allons-y!*" Mario called. " 'Urry up!" He looked enormously pleased at having said some words in English.

When the girls got back to the house, they found a message in French waiting for them. Marc translated it.

"Someone called for you," he said. "There is a number here. Would you like me to show you where the phone is?"

"I just want to wash up first," Jo said. "Come with me, Robin."

"We'll be down in a few minutes," Robin said to Marc.

The girls raced upstairs and into their room.

"Who could be calling?" Jo asked. "Do you think it's Jules?"

"If it is, we have to call when no one's around," said Robin. "I'm really beginning to worry about him."

"Let's ask Nicolette where the phone is," said Jo. "How do you say it in French?"

"I'll look it up in my little dictionary," Robin said. "Here it is. Why, it's the same word—telephone."

They went down to the breakfast room hoping to find Nicolette. She was there gathering up laundry.

"Nicolette," said Robin.

"*Oui?*" Nicolette turned her head, looked at them, and smiled.

"Telephone?" Robin asked, pantomiming a phone.

Nicolette looked puzzled.

"Telephone?" said Jo, a little louder.

Nicolette shook her head. It was obvious she didn't understand.

Robin ran upstairs and got her dictionary. She brought it down and showed Nicolette the word.

"Ah! *Téléphone,*" said Nicolette.

"Wasn't that how we said it?" Jo whispered to Robin.

Nicolette walked up the stairs and showed them the telephone in an alcove behind the sitting room.

Robin dialed the number. The ring was so different from the ones at home. This sounded like more of a buzz than a phone ringing.

Someone picked up the phone on the other end. Robin motioned Jo to come closer.

"Hello," Robin said cautiously. "Who is this?"

The voice on the other end of the line laughed.

"Robin, it hasn't been that long. This is your mother."

CHAPTER THREE

Crêpes at Midnight

"Oh, hi, Mom," Robin said. "They left us a message but they didn't tell us who called."

"Who else could it be?" her mother asked. "You don't know anyone else in Paris, do you?"

"Of course not," Robin said. She told her mother about the house and the rest of the group staying there. Her mother relayed the information to her father.

"It sounds good," said her mother. "Great talking to you, honey. Let me talk to Jo now. We'll call again soon. We love you."

While Jo talked to their parents, Robin caught her breath. She realized she had hoped the call would be from Jules. She was beginning to worry that something had happened to him.

When the sisters emerged from the hallway, they found Marc waiting for them.

"You found the phone," he said.

"Oh, yes," Robin said. "Nicolette showed us."

"Wasn't it great to talk to Mom and Dad?" Jo asked.

"Ah, it was your parents who called," Marc said.

"Ready for dinner?" Mme Georges asked.

"Could we go to the same place that we went to last night?" Jo asked.

"But we have reservations elsewhere," Mme Georges said. "It is important to experience many different types of cuisine in Paris. Tonight, we are going to a Vietnamese restaurant. You will enjoy it, I'm sure."

"But I loved that restaurant last night," Jo begged.

"Ah, well, I will try," said Mme Georges. She went to the phone and dialed a number.

Then she spoke to someone in French. She waited a moment, spoke again, and then put the phone down.

"I am sorry, *ma petite,* but the restaurant is full. I could not get a reservation. We will have to go there another night," Mme Georges said to Jo.

As they walked to the Vietnamese restaurant, Jo and Robin lagged behind.

"What are we going to do?" Jo asked.

"We'll have to ask her if we can take a walk after dinner by ourselves," Robin said.

"What if she won't let us go?" Jo asked.

"We'll have to sneak out," Robin said.

"Okay," said Jo. "I hope we have to sneak out. It'll be more exciting."

At the restaurant, Jo and Robin were absorbed in trying to figure out the French menu. Sylvie said they should try and guess since they would learn more French that way.

"What does 'p-o-r-c' mean?" Jo asked.

"Say it," said Sylvie. "What do you think it means?"

Jo tried to pronounce the word, and Sophie, giggling, said, "Oink! Oink!"

"It's pork!" Jo cried. "I'll have that."

"Very good," Sylvie said. "Now, Robin, you must choose."

"I'll have pork too," Robin said.

"No, you have to have something different," Sylvie said. "How else will you learn?"

"But I like pork," Robin said. "Okay. Either *poulet* or *boeuf.*"

"Take the *poulet*," said Marc. "You will like that."

Robin was pleased to see that when the *poulet* came, it was pieces of chicken. They munched their way through crisp spring rolls, rice, and juicy dumplings. At the end, their waiter brought a tray of oranges.

"Ooh, cold!" Jo said. The oranges were hollowed out and stuffed with tangy orange sherbet.

"No, cool," said Marc.

"You speak English really well," said Robin. "Where did you learn it?"

"In school," Marc said.

"Most of us know at least two languages besides French," Sylvie said. "We have to for university."

"What other languages do you speak?" Jo asked.

"English and Italian," said Sylvie.

"Mine are English and German," Marc said. "And Mario, poor fellow, has learned French and Russian. That's why he can't participate in our English conversations."

Mario smiled and bowed when he heard his name, then continued eating his orange ice.

"Sophie is only ten but she is beginning to learn English," Sylvie said.

Just then Sophie yawned and everyone laughed.

"Time for bed," said Mme Georges. "It's after nine-thirty. I didn't realize it was so late."

"But Mme Georges, I'm not tired," Jo said. "Could Robin and I take a walk? Please?"

"But it is late for children," said Mme Georges. "And you don't know Paris at all. I think you will be better off going back to the house with us. Tomorrow you can walk all you like. We will walk to the Louvre. That is a nice long walk," said Mme Georges, smiling.

Robin and Jo made no protest, but on the way back Robin asked Sylvie, "Do the restaurants stay open late here?"

"Of course," Sylvie said. "Some stay open all night."

"Like the one we went to last night?" Jo asked.

"That one closes about eleven or so, I think," said Sylvie. "Why do you ask? Are you still hungry?"

"I'm stuffed," said Jo. "I just wondered. This is so different from home. Everything closes by ten o'clock."

"Not in New York," Sylvie said.

"No, but we're not usually out late in New York," said Robin. "Do you think your aunt will ever let us go out alone?"

"When she is sure you will be able to find your way," Sylvie said.

"She's worse than Mom and Dad," Jo burst out. "At least they let us out of their sight now and then."

"I will talk to Aunt Amélie," Sylvie said. "Perhaps she will let you go out with me."

The girls smiled at Sylvie and Robin changed the subject. When they reached the house, they said goodnight to everyone and ran upstairs.

"Just what we need," said Jo. "Another watchdog! Sylvie!"

"She meant to be nice," Robin said. "I guess they figure it's easy to get lost here."

"We'll have to sneak out," said Jo.

"I think so," said Robin. "We'll wait until just before eleven. Maybe everyone will have gone to bed by then."

"I hope so," said Jo. "Otherwise we'll have to make up a story. How about we got hungry and were looking for some cookies or something to eat? We never get any snacks here."

"I guess that'll have to do, but they'll probably think we're pigs after the meal we ate tonight," Robin said. "If they catch us near our room, we can always say we were going to the bathroom."

The girls lay down on their beds and tried to read, but their eyes kept closing.

"I'm really tired," murmured Jo.

Robin felt herself doze off, but after a while she opened her eyes and struggled awake. She looked at the clock by her bedside. 11:05!

"Jo! Jo!" She pummeled her sister until Jo woke up.

"Wha? Whozat?" Jo mumbled.

"Come on," Robin said. "It's after eleven. We have to sneak out and go to the restaurant."

She dragged Jo up, but her sister toppled over onto the bed again. Robin yanked the pillow from under Jo's head.

"Hey! What did you do that for?" Jo cried.

"Shh! Let's go," Robin said.

Robin quietly opened the door of their room and peered out into the hall. It was totally dark. She pressed the light button in the hall.

Softly, the girls padded down the carpeted stairs. Robin strained her ears listening for sounds, but everyone seemed to be sleeping.

"This is creepy," Jo muttered.

They had almost reached the end of the staircase when the light went out abruptly. Robin stifled a scream and Jo gasped behind her. They stayed motionless for a few minutes, but no one appeared.

Finally, Robin decided it was safe to move again. They walked down the last step and moved towards the front door. The light from the street shone through the fanlight over the door, and Robin could see that nobody was in the hall or in the sitting room.

Robin tried the doorknob. It didn't move. Then she saw a lock above the keyhole. She undid the lock, opened the door slightly, and she and Jo were out.

Outside it was a different world. The street lamps and the neon lights glowed. At the sidewalk cafés, groups of people clustered around tiny tables, laughing and chattering. Couples strolled down the wide boulevard and others lined up for the giant movie theaters that advertised familiar American movies with French titles. Jo and Robin passed a pizza place and the smell of cheese and tomatoes wafted towards them. At the corner, a woman at a kiosk flipped something on a griddle.

"Pancakes!" exclaimed Jo.

"No, crêpes," said Robin. "Those thin ones are called crêpes."

Nothing looked like home. A blinking green neon cross signaled an all-night drugstore. A man walked by carrying a monkey, and a woman with red and orange hair swept across their path.

Robin and Jo would have stared all night, but Robin remembered their mission.

"We've got to go," she said. They crossed the street and ran towards the restaurant. But when they got there, the windows were dark.

"We're too late," wailed Jo. They peered through the windows. The chairs were piled on top of the tables and it looked as if the restaurant had been closed for some time.

There was a white sign on the door: *Fermeture annuelle jusqu'au 8 Août.*

"What does that mean?" Jo asked Robin.

"I don't know," she said. "I'll write it down and we'll look it up when we get back."

The girls headed back to Mme Georges's. Suddenly Robin pulled Jo into a recessed doorway. Jo started to protest, then shrank back as she saw who Robin had spotted. There on the sidewalk, striding as if she were in a great hurry, was Mme Georges. Her face was grim, without the smile it usually wore when she talked to the group.

"Where is she going?" Jo whispered.

"I don't know," said Robin. "I just hope she didn't lock the door."

"Oh, no," said Jo. "I never thought of that."

The girls raced back to the house. The door was locked.

"What are we going to do now?" Jo cried.

"We'll have to ring the bell. Wait a second." She dashed over to the woman making crêpes and held up two fingers. The woman smiled a toothless grin and spread the thin batter on a griddle. She flipped it over when the underside was brown and sprinkled sugar on it. Then she folded the whole thing up as if it were a handkerchief and slid it into a thin waxed paper envelope, and repeated the procedure for the second crêpe.

"It's good thing I had some money in my pocket," Robin said. She handed one of the steaming pancakes to her sister.

Then she rang the bell.

"Let me do the talking," she said.

They could hear heavy footsteps thumping down the hall. Finally, Nicolette opened the door. She was dressed in a bathrobe and slippers and had a nightcap on her head.

Her eyes opened wide when she saw Robin and Jo. She started scolding them in French and pulling them inside at the same time.

"We were so hungry," Robin said. She showed Nicolette her crêpe.

Jo smiled sweetly at Nicolette and kissed her. Nicolette smiled back and patted Jo on the cheek.

"*Allons-y*," she said, shooing them upstairs. Then, shaking her head, she shuffled back to her bedroom.

"That was close," said Jo. "I'm glad you thought of those crêpes. They're pretty good, too." She took a big bite out of hers.

"Still, we'd better be prepared to make up some story for tomorrow if Nicolette decides to tell Mme Georges," Robin said. She took her little French book out of her bag and turned the pages impatiently. Finally, she found the section she was looking for.

"*Fermeture,*" she said. "It means 'shutting, close, closing.'"

"And '*jusqu'au*'?" asked Jo.

"That means 'until,' and '*Août*' is August."

"Hmm. Closing until August 8," Robin said. "That means . . ."

"That the restaurant was closed," said Jo. "We weren't too late after all. It just wasn't open."

"Right. It wasn't open today at all," said Robin. "And if it wasn't open, where is Jules? And who was Mme Georges talking to when she said we couldn't get a reservation, that the restaurant was full?"

"Maybe she got a wrong number?" Jo said.

"I don't think so," Robin said. "I think something's wrong here, and I think Mme Georges lied to us."

The Radish Man

The next morning, Robin and Jo went into the breakfast room cautiously. Had Nicolette told Mme Georges she had let them in last night? What would Mme Georges say?

They slid into their seats after saying good morning to everyone. Nothing seemed different. Nicolette came trudging out of the kitchen loaded down with hot chocolate and croissants. Jo looked at her anxiously, but Nicolette responded with a big smile and a wink. Then she slipped Jo an extra croissant.

"This morning we go to the Louvre," said Mme Georges.

Sophie pouted, but everyone else looked pleased at the prospect.

"If Sophie does not want to go, Sylvie, you may take her to the Jardin du Luxembourg to play," said Mme Georges.

"Bon," said Sylvie, and she took Sophie by the hand and they left the breakfast room.

Robin and Jo went up to their room to get ready. Jo picked up her backpack.

"Are you going to take that with you?" asked Robin.

"Sure," said Jo.

"Do you still have the package from Jules in it?" Robin asked. "Maybe we'd better hide it someplace."

"It's probably safer with me," Jo said.

"I don't think so," said Robin. "Here's a good spot, in the closet behind your old sneakers. Anybody who could stand that smell can have the package!"

"I can't help it!" cried Jo. "Mom won't buy me new ones until these wear out."

"Never mind," said Robin. "When Mom and Dad get back from Cannes, I'll convince them. That smell is more than I can stand!"

Jo pouted all the way downstairs, but her mood lifted when they got outside. The woman cooking crêpes had vanished from the corner. In her place was a man sitting on a wooden box. An old, battered, brown hat was tilted over his face. At his feet were a tin cup and a sign: "*Je n'ai plus un radis.*"

"What does that mean?" Robin asked Marc.

"Well, it's a slang expression. Properly, it means 'I don't have a radish.'"

"How funny," Jo said.

"But in slang it means 'I am completely broke.'"

"I like that," Jo said. She darted back to place a coin in the cup.

"Your sister has a kind heart," Marc said to Robin.

"I felt sorry for the radish man," Jo explained.

The sun blazed from the tiled roofs and sparkled off the glass windows of the stores as they walked down the narrow streets to the river. Jo bounced along for a while, but as they walked beside the Seine, Robin noticed her energy flagging. It was a long walk in the heat.

"Perhaps we can rest for a minute," she suggested to Mme Georges.

"Nonsense," she replied. "Children need exercise."

Eventually everyone was dragging except Marc and Mme Georges. At last they came to a massive cobblestoned courtyard, across which Robin saw the huge, pale yellow buildings of the Louvre and the gleaming glass pyramid in front of them.

"It's magnificent," said Robin, her mouth dropping open.

"It was a palace in the fourteenth century," said Marc. "Ever since then, we French have worked to make it more beautiful."

"But that pyramid's not old," said Jo.

"No," said Marc. "Remember I said we continue to work to make the Louvre more beautiful? This is something modern we added. It's by the great architect I. M. Pei."

"Come," said Mme Georges. "We will enter through the carrousel."

"A carrousel!" Jo cried. "Can I get a ride on it?"

"We will see," said Mme Georges. They walked down stone steps and entered an area filled with shops.

"Where's the carrousel?" asked Jo, looking around.

"Oh, now I understand," said Marc. "You thought it was one of those things that have horses and play tunes. No, this carrousel is simply an entrance to the museum."

"Then why do they call it a carrousel?" Robin asked.

"Perhaps because the main area is round with hallways leading off from it," said Marc.

"French is certainly a funny language," said Jo.

"I don't know about that," said Marc. "English is pretty funny, too. Like what do you call sausages—hot dogs? Are they made from dogs?"

"Of course not," said Jo. "We call them hot dogs because . . . well, because they're hot dogs."

Robin bit back a smile as she listened to them. She looked around the great hall and glanced at the gleaming walls. It felt as if she were inside a smooth yellow marble. Then she looked up and saw the pyramid.

"It looks like a game of jacks," Jo cried. Seen from the inside the pyramid did indeed look like the game pieces. Through the glass, they could see another part of the old building and a huge fountain.

"I have tickets, so we will not have to wait in line," said Mme Georges. Robin saw that other tourists were standing in huge lines, waiting to buy tickets to get in.

Two staircases and an escalator fanned out from the center of the hall. Robin saw there were three choices of which parts of the Louvre they could go to: Sully, Richelieu, or Denon.

"Everyone must see the Mona Lisa first," said Mme Georges. She herded them towards a huge staircase and gestured towards a statue at the top. "That is Winged Victory, very famous."

As they trudged up the stairs, Robin looked through the window. Outside people were sitting next to the fountain, dunking their feet, and sunbathing. Others lounged under the yellow umbrellas of the café.

Finally, they entered the room where the Mona Lisa was mounted. It was hot. People flapped their brochures like fans for a breath of cool air. Yet crowds pressed around the painting. Enclosed in a special display case of pale brown, behind bullet-proof glass, was one of the most famous paintings in the world.

"Is that it?" asked Jo. She stood on tiptoe to see the portrait of the smooth-faced woman with the faint smile.

"You don't seem very impressed," Marc said.

"No, I'm not," said Jo. "I thought it would be more special."

"Watch what happens when you walk away," he said.

"Her eyes are following me," said Jo. "That's weird."

She and Robin and Mario wandered over to an enormous painting filled with men and women at a long table. Marc joined them. Mme Georges was still surveying the Mona Lisa.

"It looks like a party," Jo said.

"It is. It's from the Bible," said Marc. "It's a wedding feast."

Robin admired the bold figures and the bright colors. But as they strolled from gallery to gallery, she started to feel hot and tired.

"Do you think we'll be going back soon?" she asked. "I could use a cold drink and a rest."

"Soon, I think," Marc said. "Oh, look, here's the painting there was all that fuss about."

He pointed to a small painting of a woman. Her hair was parted in the middle and pulled tightly back off her head. She had a half smile on her red lips. A white fur was draped around her arms, and she wore a white dress with short puffed sleeves. In the background were a river, trees, and the faint spire of a church.

"It's lovely, but what do you mean 'fuss'?" Robin asked.

"There were two paintings," Marc said. "Didn't you read about it in the States? It was all over the papers here."

"I must have missed it," said Robin.

"She never reads the newspapers," Jo chimed in. "Just fashion magazines."

"Ignore her," said Robin. "Tell me about it."

"There was a much smaller version of this one, a miniature, that a wealthy couple owned," he said. "They kept it in their *château* in the Loire Valley."

"What's a *château?*" Jo asked.

"A castle," Marc said. "The Loire Valley is full of them."

"Cool. You have castles here? Can we see one?" Jo asked.

"They're an hour or two away from here," Marc said. "Anyway, the couple went to their *château* for the weekend, and found the little painting had been stolen. No one has seen it since."

"Somebody must have liked it a lot," Jo said.

"It's worth a great deal of money," Marc said. "And it's not the only painting that's been stolen from these *châteaux*. There've been many this past year. The police think a gang of thieves has been doing this, and they bring the stolen paintings to Paris and ship them out of the country."

"How big was the little painting?" Robin asked.

Marc gestured with his hands. "About this big," he said.

Mme Georges turned from contemplating a painting and clapped her hands.

"*Bien, mes enfants,* okay, children, time to go," she said. "The good Nicolette will have lunch for us."

"Do we have to walk back?" Jo asked, dragging her feet.

"I thought you enjoyed walking," Mme Georges said. "No, I think we will take the métro back."

On the way home, Jo chattered with Marc while Mme Georges and Mario conversed in Italian. Robin sat lost in thought until Jo poked her when they came to their stop.

"The radish man doesn't seem to have made any more money," said Jo as they passed the beggar. His tin cup appeared to be empty, but he had a half-empty bottle of wine cradled in his arm.

"He's probably already spent what he made this morning on that wine," Marc said.

"Good-bye, radish man," Jo called, before they entered the house.

Robin looked back and saw the man stare at Jo for a minute before he closed his eyes again.

At lunch, Robin ate her quiche quickly. She noticed that Jo ate hers too, even though ordinarily she might have been suspicious of the cheese and ham pie. She must have been hungry, Robin thought. Dessert was fruit, and Robin asked to be excused. She pulled Jo along with her as she left the table.

"Do not take too long," called Mme Georges. "This afternoon, we visit the perfume museum. I know you will like that."

She turned to Sylvie. "And you will go with us?"

"Yes. I love the perfume museum. You will enjoy it," she said to Robin and Jo.

"Alas, I am busy this afternoon," said Marc.

"Ah, and will you take Mario with you?" asked Mme Georges. "I think he will be too busy for perfume as well."

When they were back in their room, Jo said, "What's the rush?"

"I've had an idea," Robin said. "Let's open the package from Jules."

"But he hasn't come back. How can we open it? It isn't ours," Jo said.

"I don't think we can wait for Jules. I think something might have happened to him," Robin said.

Jo whimpered. "You're scaring me."

Robin took a deep breath. "There's nothing to be scared about. I just want to see what's in that package."

She watched Jo rummage around and drag out her sneakers. Then Jo felt behind them and drew out the little package.

Robin measured it with her hands. "It looks about right," she muttered.

"Right for what?" Jo cried.

"Shh! We don't want Mme Georges up here asking what's the matter."

Robin tried to untie the rough brown twine around the package, but it was too tough for her fingers.

"Where are the nail scissors?" she asked.

"I don't know," said Jo. "You had them last."

"I gave them to you," Robin said.

"Did not," said Jo, sticking out her lower lip.

"Let's not fight about this. How are we going to get this package open?"

"I'll run down to Nicolette and ask her for a pair of scissors," Jo said.

"Okay, but make it fast," Robin said. "We're supposed to go to the perfume museum soon."

Robin paced anxiously around the room, while Jo ran downstairs. She kept glancing at her watch. Mme Georges could call them at any time.

Finally, she heard Jo's footsteps returning.

Robin opened the door and hissed, "Did you get them?"

Jo held up the scissors triumphantly in one hand, two cookies in the other.

"I told you to get scissors, not stuff yourself," Robin said.

"Can I help it if Nicolette thinks I'm starving and wants to give me food?" Jo said smugly.

Robin clipped the twine and opened the brown paper wrapping. "It looks like the back of a picture," Robin said. Holding her breath, she turned it right side up.

There, facing the girls, was a small black frame enclosing a wrinkled map of Paris.

Someone in the Room

 "Robin! Jo! Are you ready?" Mme Georges's voice floated up the staircase.

"Coming," Robin cried. She hurriedly wrapped the map back in the brown paper and thrust it behind the sneakers again.

Jo scowled. "All that for an old map," she said. "Big secret. Big deal."

"Let's go," said Robin. "I don't think we have to worry about Jules anymore."

"He must have been playing a joke on us," Jo said. "We fell for it."

They scrambled down the stairs to find Mme Georges, Sophie, and Sylvie waiting for them.

"I am not feeling so well," Mme Georges said, pressing her hand to her forehead. "Sylvie will take you to the perfume museum."

"I'm sorry," said Robin.

"It's these headaches I get," Mme Georges said. "They are terrible. But tonight I will be better. We have a dinner near the Eiffel Tower and then you can see it. It is very beautiful at night."

"That sounds great," said Jo loudly.

Mme Georges winced. "I will take a nap now. What is it you

Americans say? Ah, have a nice day." She wandered off to her room, waving good-bye limply.

"Very well," said Sylvie, "we will go now."

"It's not too much trouble, is it?" asked Robin.

"Of course not," the girl said. She took Sophie firmly by the hand and they left the house.

The perfume museum was in a small building on a street lined with offices and hotels. Its narrow entrance hall led to a long staircase. The girls walked up the creaky wooden stairs and into a huge, yellow room decorated with white plaster. A large mirror framed in gold hung on one wall. The rest of the room was crammed with display cases.

"Wow!" said Jo, looking around at all the space.

"Look at the copper pots they used to make the perfume," Sylvie said. Jo and Sophie leaned over to look inside and Sophie nearly tumbled in.

"Watch out!" Jo exclaimed and pulled the little girl back.

"*Merci,*" she said, smiling at Jo.

The girls were enchanted with the old perfume bottles in the glass cases of the museum.

"Look, there's one shaped like a boy with a dog," Robin said.

"I like the little traveling kits," said Sylvie. "They're from the seventeen hundreds. I'm always amazed they could use those tiny nail brushes and nail files and the miniature scissors."

"Maybe people had smaller hands then," Robin said.

"I like the beauty spots," Jo said. She stared at the little black patches that women put on their faces as decoration.

"Eeek! A ghost!" yelled Jo.

Sophie jumped and then she laughed when she saw what Jo was pointing to. There were two perfume bottles shaped like ghosts, one painted black, one white. The white one had red eyes.

"There are so many old things in Paris," Robin said.

"Yes, and many of them are very valuable," said Sylvie.

"What about maps?" Robin asked.

"Oh, yes, there are many ancient maps that are worth money," Sylvie answered.

"How would you find out if one were valuable?" Robin asked.

"Why do you ask?" Sylvie said.

"My father collects maps, and I might want to buy him one as a present," she said.

"Ah, well, perhaps we will go to the Marché aux Puces, the flea market, on Sunday, and we can look there," Sylvie said. "There are some map sellers there."

"A flea market?" Jo wrinkled her nose. "Do they sell valuable things there?"

"Oh, yes, do not let the name fool you," Sylvie replied. "There are many antiques sold there."

"Do you know a lot about antiques?" Robin asked.

"We used to have many before my parents died," Sylvie said. "Then they were sold."

"Did you go to live with your aunt after your parents died?" Jo asked.

Sylvie hesitated, and Robin noticed the sad expression that came over the young woman's face.

"You don't have to talk about it," Robin said. "Sometimes my sister is too nosy. I'm sorry."

Jo began to protest, but Sylvie said quickly, "No, no. There is nothing to be sorry about. Yes, after my parents died, Aunt Amélie took me in. Of course, she's not my real aunt, but she likes me to call her that. She was a friend of my parents."

The girls drifted to a large, three-sided piece of wooden furniture.

"Ah, this is the *pièce de résistance,*" said Sylvie.

"English, please," said Jo.

"The most amazing thing here," said Sylvie.

"It looks pretty amazing to me," said Robin. "What is it?"

"It's called a perfume organ," Sylvie said.

"Do they play music on it?" Jo asked.

"No, it's called an organ because just like music is composed, so are perfumes," Sylvie answered. She pointed to the seven tiers filled with bottles.

"Does it take that many bottles to make a perfume?" asked Robin. "That's hard to believe."

"Not that many," said Sylvie, "but a lot. Come downstairs and you'll see my favorite part."

When Robin and Jo bounded down the stairs, they could see why the big room with the brown tiled floor was Sylvie's favorite. Bottles of perfume were stacked on shelves. Young women held up perfume to spray on customers or provided them with sticks dipped into the perfumes. Customers rubbed those on their wrists.

Robin and Jo rushed to the gleaming yellow metal bottles and tried the scents.

"I like this one," Jo said.

"That is Miranda," said the saleswoman. "It is made of vanilla and coconut."

"It sounds more like it should be candy," said Jo, sniffing. "But it sure smells great."

Robin chose one made of white flowers and watermelon.

"Its name is Dahlia. Isn't that cool?" she asked Sylvie.

Then with Sylvie's help, they chose a perfume for their mother and some cologne for their father. While they shopped, Sophie ran around the room trying the testing sticks. All the saleswomen cooed over her.

"What about you, Sylvie?" Robin asked.

"I have plenty of perfume," the girl answered. But Robin noticed that Sylvie looked longingly at the bottles before she turned away.

"We can have a drink now," Sylvie said, as they came out of the museum.

Robin wiped her forehead and Jo fanned herself. It was still hot even though it was almost four o'clock in the afternoon.

"Definitely," said Jo. "I could use something to drink."

"I have someplace special to take you," said Sylvie.

After another long walk they reached a large department store whose name, Samaritaine, was emblazoned across the front of the building.

"This doesn't look much like a place to get a drink," Jo said, staring at the huge windows filled with clothing.

"It's one of the best places in Paris," Sylvie said. "Follow me."

Robin felt so hot and tired from walking that she didn't even pay attention to the clothes. Sylvie led them inside, past crowded cosmetics counters, and to a bank of elevators. They got into an elevator and she pressed a button. When they reached their floor, she told them to walk up a little iron staircase that was there. Finally, they opened a door and walked out onto a roof.

"*Voilà!*" cried Sylvie.

Sophie ran to the edge of the roof and hung over the railing. She pointed to the view and chattered to Sylvie. Robin and Jo walked around the roof, where people were sitting at tables under umbrellas and eating and drinking.

"You can see all of Paris here," Robin said. She gazed at hills covered with buildings, at the gold dome of a church rising in the distance, and, farther away, the tall towers of skyscrapers. She was content to look at the view for a long time.

At last, the girls settled happily at a little table with ice cream and drinks. Jo fanned herself in the warm air.

"Don't they have air conditioning in France?" she asked.

"It's not so popular here," Sylvie said. "Mostly the expensive restaurants and hotels have it. It doesn't get that hot in Paris."

"I'm cooling off now," said Robin, as she drank her iced soda.

Sylvie, she noticed, had ordered coffee, saying, "Parisians can drink coffee anytime."

Robin sucked up the last of her drink through her straw and stared off into the distance. Sophie drooped over her plate of ice cream.

"We should go back," said Sylvie.

As they left, Robin took one last look.

"This is beautiful, Sylvie. Thank you for showing it to us," she said.

"When I need peace and quiet and I want to get away from things, I come here," said Sylvie. "Particularly when I'm feeling bad."

"Do you feel bad often?" Robin asked.

Sylvie shook her head, and turned to help Sophie cross the street.

Robin realized the conversation was over, and began walking with Jo, who had regained her energy and was bouncing down the street. When they reached their corner, she pointed out all the things that told her they were coming to Mme Georges's.

"There's the drugstore with the green cross, and there's the pastry shop, and the shoe store and the . . ." She stopped and looked around.

"The radish man is gone," she said.

"Who?" Sylvie asked.

Robin and Jo explained the radish man to her. Sylvie looked amused.

"He probably collected enough money here and went to drink it up," Sylvie said. "There are what you call 'radish men' all over Paris."

Jo cast a last glance at the corner where the man had perched, and went into the house. It was quiet except for the hum of Nicolette's vacuum cleaner.

"Nicolette!" Sylvie cried. Nicolette appeared, carrying the hose for the vacuum.

"I will ask her if the boys have come back," she explained to Jo and Robin. She and Nicolette conversed for a few minutes, then the older woman went back to her work.

"She says they are still out and that my aunt is sleeping. Sophie looks like she could use a nap, but we have some time before dinner. What would you like to do now?"

The girls agreed they would play some kind of board game, and giggled to see Sylvie pull out a battered Monopoly game. They laughed even more when they saw that the properties all had French names.

"Rue de la Paix," said Jo. "That's the same color as Boardwalk at home. That must be an expensive one."

They played until Mario and Marc came in, hot and tired.

"Where did you two go?" Jo asked.

"We played soccer in the park," Marc said.

"Who won?" Sylvie asked, smiling.

"Our side, of course," said Marc. He translated for Mario who clasped his hands over his head and shook them to signal victory.

The boys joined in the Monopoly game and they played sides, girls against the boys, until Mme Georges strolled in.

"It is late," she said, tapping her watch. She surveyed Marc and Mario.

"You need to clean yourselves before we go out," she said.

"Is your headache better, Madame?" Robin asked.

"My headache?" Mme Georges looked vague. "Oh, yes, my headache. Much better, thank you."

"I'll just go and clean up," said Robin.

"You are fine the way you are," said Mme Georges. "You and your sister always look pretty."

"Thank you, but I need to wash my face," said Robin. "I feel hot and sweaty."

"Very well," said Mme Georges. "But all of you . . . hurry now. We don't want to be late for dinner. It is cheese fondue tonight."

Jo grumbled as they went up the stairs.

"Yuck . . . cheese . . . I'd give anything for a big juicy hamburger or some pizza," she said.

"Fondue is almost like pizza," Robin said. "Melted cheese without the tomatoes."

"It's not the same at all, and you know it, Robin Bridge," Jo replied.

"At least she hasn't made you eat snails yet," Robin said.

"And she'd better not!" Jo flung open the door to their room.

Robin looked around for her washcloth and her hairbrush.

"That's funny. I thought I left my hairbrush on the dresser. Now it's on the desk," she said.

She opened the drawers of her dresser and gasped.

"What is it?" Jo asked.

"I always put my diary on the bottom of the drawer, beneath my underwear. Now it's on top."

She turned to her sister and said, "I think someone's been searching our room."

CHAPTER SIX

Trouble in the Métro

"You're right!" exclaimed Jo, who had immediately pulled open a drawer in the dresser she was using. "I put my pajamas on top so I can get to them fast at night. Now they're at the bottom. Is the map still there?"

Robin went to the closet and plunged her hand behind the sneakers. "Yes. I can't understand what's going on here."

She took the picture out and held it up. "I can't see anything unusual about this map, can you?"

"It looks like the maps that Mme Georges gave us in case we got lost," said Jo, sitting down on the bed with it. "Not that we've had the chance."

She examined the frame again and turned it over.

"Robin! Jo! We are waiting for you," came the call from Mme Georges.

"Coming!" Robin yelled. She turned to Jo.

"Who do you think searched our room?" she asked.

"It could be anybody," Jo said.

"The boys could have done it," said Robin. "Mme Georges was home all day. The only people we know who couldn't have done it were Sylvie and Sophie. They were with us."

"I don't think Mario would do it," said Jo. "After all, he can't even speak English."

"He doesn't need to know English to search our room," said Robin.

"But what would Mario be looking for?" Jo asked. She plunged the picture back behind her sneakers.

"Jo! Robin!" The cry was louder now and more insistent.

"Let's go," said Robin, "but let's be suspicious of everyone."

Later, over the bubbling pots of cheese in the fondue restaurant, Robin looked around. There was Sophie laughing as she lost her crust of bread in the pot. Mario successfully pulled his piece out with a long fork and expertly twirled the hot cheese around his bread. Marc and Jo were threading lots of pieces of bread on their forks in an attempt to get as much as they could, while Sylvie smiled and Mme Georges looked on indulgently.

Which of them could have searched the room? Robin's head whirled with possibilities.

"You're not eating, Robin," said Sylvie, watching her carefully.

"There's too much competition," Robin said, laughing as she tried to stick her fork into the crowded pot.

After chocolate mousse, or pudding, the group took the métro to the Eiffel Tower.

"This is amazing," said Jo, as she gazed up at the huge, brown, steel construction. In the distance, she could see a long, sandy walkway and a green field, but the whole area was dominated by the Eiffel Tower. They walked under it and stared at its huge legs.

"I feel like an ant beneath it. Is the Eiffel Tower the world's tallest building?" Jo asked.

"No," said Marc, "but it is old and big. It was built by Gustave Eiffel for the 1889 World Exposition in Paris. And it's made of ten thousand tons of metal."

"Let's go up," said Mme Georges. She bought tickets and led the group to a red cage that turned out to be the elevator.

"I am sorry," she said to Robin and Jo as they ascended. "The top is closed. We will go to the second floor."

"I wanted to go to the very top," Jo said.

"Never mind," said Mme Georges. "You will be at a great height. Our second floor is your third floor. It may be enough for you. Now remember, if we get separated, we will meet downstairs at the ticket office."

They left the elevator and walked to the railing. The second floor was crammed with people and the girls had to maneuver their way through the crowd carefully.

Robin looked over the railing.

"You can see the river and the bridges," Jo said.

"The cars look so tiny on the street," Robin remarked. Her knees felt weak as she looked down.

The girls walked around to the other side.

"There are people picnicking on the grass," Jo remarked.

"Let's go downstairs," said Robin.

Jo and Robin walked down narrow, yellow, metal stairs to the first floor. Robin sighed with relief. Here, the railing was fenced in with wire that climbed high up it.

"I can't believe it!" she cried, as she looked at the railing.

"Rocio de Mingo," read Jo. "I love Niko. España. There's graffiti written all over this fence."

"I can't believe that people would do that to such a beautiful building," Robin said.

She looked around and realized they had lost the others.

"Where are Mme Georges and the rest?" she asked Jo.

"I think they're still upstairs on the second floor," she said.

"My knees feel weak," said Robin. "I'd like to go down."

"Let's wait for them below," said Jo. "We can meet them at the ticket office. Besides, there's a little park I'd like to look at before we go back."

When the girls had descended, they looked up to see the tower lit for the evening. The brown metal glowed like gold in the soft lights.

"They're not at the ticket office yet," Robin said.

"Good," said Jo, "we can walk around the little park." She headed off to the left of the tower to a dark corner filled with trees and plants.

"Isn't this pretty?" she said.

The girls strolled around the park, admiring the tall trees and the bushes.

"I was a little worried about this, but it seems to be safe," Robin said. Other people walked near them and there was a wide, well-lit street nearby.

"Yow!" Robin jumped as a man came out of a dark spot behind a tree and ran up to them.

"Jules!" cried Jo, recognizing the waiter. "Where have you been?"

"We've been looking for you everywhere!" Robin exclaimed.

"You have not told anyone about the package?" Jules asked.

"No, but some strange things have been happening," Robin said. "Is it dangerous?"

"Not to you," Jules said quickly. "I need the package. Where is it?"

"At Mme Georges's," Jo said. "You can come and pick it up tonight."

"That is impossible," Jules said. "I wish to ask you another favor."

Two little boys ran by yelling, and the waiter jumped. He looked around carefully.

"I wish you to bring the package to a place for me," he said.

"I don't know how we can do that," Robin said. "Mme Georges doesn't let us go out on our own. Perhaps we could ask her to go with us or maybe Sylvie or Marc would."

"No!" Jules said sharply. "You must bring it on your own."

Just then, Mario came running up to the girls.

"*Allons-y!* 'Urry up," he said, taking Jo's hand. He pointed in the direction of the ticket office.

Robin and Jo turned back to talk to Jules, but he had melted into the darkness. As they walked back with Mario, Robin motioned to Jo that they would talk about Jules later.

When they reached the group, Mme Georges asked, "Where were you?"

"We went for a walk in that pretty little park," Jo said.

"It is not a good idea to go off by yourselves," Mme Georges said. "Not everyone is nice in Paris."

But Jo's attention was distracted by a mime, painted gold and draped in golden cloth to resemble a mummy, who was performing near the entrance to the tower.

She ran over to see him, weaving through the booths of vendors selling caps and T-shirts. Robin's eye was caught by a man selling miniature Eiffel Towers.

"I'd like to have one of those to take back home," she said to Marc.

He helped her negotiate for the souvenir and they watched as the man wrapped it up in a bag.

After Jo had had her fill of staring at the mime, the group crossed the street, ready to take the métro back, when Jo spied something else.

"It's a carrousel," she said. "A real one. Can we take a ride?"

The lights of the merry-go-round twinkled and the tune was irresistible. Sophie looked up with pleading eyes at Mme Georges, and Sylvie talked to her aunt in a low, insistent tone.

"Oh, very well," said Mme Georges, grudgingly. "But we must leave soon."

Everyone except Mme Georges hopped on for a ride. Sophie clutched the carved mane of a brown stallion, while Jo sat astride a white mare. Sylvie and Robin settled themselves in a gilded coach and kept an eye on the younger girls.

"Sometimes my aunt forgets what it's like to be young," Sylvie said. "She is so concerned with making money, she doesn't think about fun."

"Money? She has that nice house, and that big diamond ring," Robin said. "She's certainly not poor."

"But she is not rich," Sylvie said. "She works hard for her money. The diamond is from her husband, but she is no longer with him."

"Are they divorced?" Robin asked.

"No, but they do not live together," Sylvie said.

A blare of music drowned out whatever else Sylvie had started to say. The merry-go-round began revolving and Jo and Sophie shrieked with delight as they went up and down and around. Robin thought about Jules again, and what he had wanted. She shivered. This was beginning to seem like something she and her sister should not be involved in. She stared into the distance, where she could see the Eiffel Tower, proud and majestic, shining like a great beacon.

"How will I ever be able to describe this when I get home?" she thought, and forgot about Jules.

When the ride ended, they scrambled off and bought huge sticks of pink cotton candy. Robin could see that Jo was in heaven as she bit off hunks of the sugary treat.

She put her arm around her sister as they plodded down the huge steps to the métro, pulled here and there by the crowd.

"Everyone is going home at the same time," Mme Georges grumbled. "We should have left earlier."

Jo laughed as she put her métro ticket into the slot next to the turnstile and it immediately shot up again.

"Don't forget to take it," warned Sylvie.

"Does anybody really look at it when you leave the station?" Jo asked.

"Not usually," Sylvie admitted, "but once friends of mine threw theirs away and then the inspector asked to see them. He didn't believe that they had bought tickets so he made them pay all over again."

Robin held on tight to her ticket. The crowd grew bigger and more insistent as the train came roaring into the station. She grabbed Jo's hand, determined not to be separated from her sister.

The car doors opened. As they moved towards the same car as their group, a man pushed them to the side and the crowd swept them into another car.

"Do you know where to get off?" Jo asked her sister.

"Yes, our stop is Odeon," said Robin. "Don't worry."

Once inside the car, the girls jumped as Jules appeared beside them all of a sudden.

"Did you push us in here?" Robin demanded.

"I had to see you alone," he said.

"We're not going anyplace," Robin said. She clutched Jo tightly.

"You do not have to go now. Simply meet me at Notre-Dame at ten in the morning on Tuesday. It is not so far from where you are staying. You can say you want to go to the mass. Bring the package. Please, please, this is very important," Jules said. The train stopped and he lurched out the door with the rest of the crowd.

Robin and Jo sank into empty seats on the train. There were far fewer people now in the car and the girls were the youngest passengers.

"That was creepy," Jo said. "Do you think we should go to Notre-Dame on Tuesday?"

"I don't know what to do," Robin said. "He certainly looked frightened to death."

"That's for sure. He never stopped twitching," Jo said.

"I'm just worried about this," said Robin. "Maybe we should call Mom and Dad."

"No! They'll probably cut their trip short and yank us away from Mme Georges's," Jo shrieked.

"I am having a good time," Robin said. "Let's think about it."

She looked out the window and saw the sign for their stop flashing.

"Here we are," she said. No other passengers were leaving. The girls waited for the door to open. Nothing happened.

"Maybe it's stuck," said Jo.

The girls hammered on the door. They could see Mme Georges and the rest of the group waiting for them at the foot of the stairs. The door remained closed.

With a heave, the train started up again. The station flashed by and Jo and Robin looked at each other.

"What do we do now?" Jo asked.

"I have no idea," said Robin. "No idea at all."

CHAPTER SEVEN

For the Birds

 The girls stared at the métro car door as the train glided swiftly into the next station.

"What do we do now?" Jo asked again.

A man shouldered her aside as the train shuddered to a stop.

"Look," said Robin. The man flipped a little handle back and pushed the door open. The girls, close on his heels, followed him out into the station.

"I didn't know you had to open some of the métro doors by hand," Robin said. "I thought they opened automatically, like they do at home."

"I'm glad we finally got out," Jo said. "I was beginning to worry."

"Now all we have to do is figure out how to get back," Robin remarked.

"That should be easy. We'll go look at the map," Jo said.

They found the map, but it was one that didn't light up the route. Some places were so worn it was impossible to read the names.

"All we have to do is go back one stop," said Robin.

"But in what direction?" Jo asked. They faced two corridors, each marked with the name of the last stop of the train. Finally, they managed to figure out which way they needed to go with the help of their little pocket métro maps.

"It's this way," Robin said. They began walking up and down stairs in a long, white-tiled corridor. It was late, but a number of couples strolled past them, as well as a few men with a harried air.

They made a turn and they were alone in the passage. The light was dim and their footsteps echoed loudly.

"Eeee!" The noise made the girls jump. Three boys came running past, leaping down the stairs and landing in front of them. One grinned back at Jo and Robin as he raced by.

Jo clutched Robin. "I don't think I like Paris as much as I did," she said.

"Don't worry," Robin responded, "they're just jerks. They won't hurt us."

They walked on and soon came to the platform, where the boys were playing tag with each other, while an older couple frowned at them. As the train pulled into the station, Robin was careful to get into a different car from the boys.

"Are you sure this is the right way?" Jo asked Robin.

"Absolutely," said Robin, crossing her fingers when Jo wasn't looking. She scanned the sign inside the train, but someone had scribbled over it so it was hard to make out the métro stops.

Whoosh! The train had stopped. Odeon! It was the right stop. Robin sighed, unlatched the handle and pushed the door with all her might.

"We're here! Yay!" Jo danced on the platform.

Marc came running down the stairs.

"They're here! What happened to you?" he asked.

Mme Georges followed him.

"Where did you girls go?" she scolded. "You must stay with the group. I am responsible for you. You girls are wild. No discipline. Just like all Americans. Our French children know how to behave. . . ." She kept on yelling at them.

Robin saw Jo's lip tremble. She knew that no one had ever yelled at Jo like that before. Robin put her arm around her sister and raised her voice.

"Excuse me, Mme Georges, but we were pushed away from the group by the crowd. Then we didn't know that the métro door didn't open automatically. We were just as worried as you were. Believe me, this wasn't any fun for us," she said. "Now, I think we'd better go back. It's very late."

Mme Georges shot her a dirty look, but stopped yelling and turned on her heel. They walked up the stairs to where Sylvie waited with the others.

"What happened?" Sylvie whispered, as Mme Georges stalked on ahead.

Robin told her and Jo added, "Your aunt yelled at us. I think she's very unfair."

"She was terribly worried, and when she is, sometimes she is mean," Sylvie said.

"But Robin told her off," Jo said, smiling.

"You are very brave," Sylvie said. "I would never dare to do such a thing."

"I'm used to it. My history teacher yells like that so I've

gotten so I never pay any attention. It doesn't bother me anymore."

That night, before they got into bed, Robin said, "I don't think we should just wait around until Tuesday. I think we should do something."

"Like what?" Jo asked, buttoning her pajamas.

"There must be more to the map than we think," said Robin. "Let's look at it again."

Carefully, the girls inspected the map.

"There is something," said Robin. "There's a tiny dot by Notre-Dame."

"Jules asked us to meet him there," Jo said. "There must be something important about it."

Robin took out her guidebook. "It's one of the best-known churches in the world," she read. "It was built between 1163 and 1361. There are three famous stained glass windows called the 'rose' windows. Victor Hugo wrote about it in *The Hunchback of Notre Dame*."

"I saw that," Jo said, excitedly. "That's the one where he lives in the bell tower and he rescues Esmeralda. I didn't realize it was a real place. Cool. I want to go there."

"I don't see any reason why we shouldn't," Robin said, "but maybe we should have an expert look at the map first, before we just hand it over to Jules. He seems to want it badly, and I'd like to know why."

"How will we do that?" Jo asked.

"Tomorrow's Sunday. My guidebook says that the flea market is open tomorrow. Let's ask Mme Georges if we can go," Robin said.

"I don't want to ask her anything," Jo pouted. "She's horrible."

"I agree. Maybe we can ask Sylvie to ask her," Robin said, as she snuggled down under the covers.

But the next morning, Mme Georges greeted the girls brightly, as if the scene in the métro station had never taken place.

"*Bonjour,*" she said, sweetly. "Did you girls sleep well?"

Jo mumbled something, but Robin faced her boldly and said, "Fine, thank you."

As the group chatted over their usual flaky pastries and sweet hot chocolate, Robin, her heart pounding, asked, "Can we go to the flea market today, Mme Georges? I have presents to buy for my family."

"*Bien sûr,*" Mme Georges said, with a faint smile. "First, we will go to another kind of market, the bird market. That will be great fun for you. Then we will go to the Marché aux Puces, the flea market."

As the group walked up the broad avenue flanked by sidewalk cafés and leafy trees, Robin and Jo lagged behind.

"Mme Georges is so weird," Jo complained. "Last night, she was screaming her head off. Today, she's as nice as can be. Do you think she's nuts?"

"No, I think that maybe she's sorry for what she did, but she can't apologize to kids so she's just trying to pretend as if it never happened," Robin said. "I think we should try to forget it, too."

"Try to forget what?" asked Marc, dropping back to walk with them.

"That—" Jo started to complain, but Robin dug her elbow into her sister's arm.

"Ow!" Jo rubbed her arm and glared at Robin.

"I'm sorry," Robin said. "I almost tripped on the cobblestones and I must have hit you."

"The cobblestones have an ancient history here," Marc said. "Sometimes, when the crowds were facing the police or the king's army and had no weapons, they pried up the cobblestones and threw them. A well-aimed cobblestone could do a lot of damage."

"I bet," Robin said. Then she heard a twittering sound. As they drew closer, it got louder and louder.

Jo ran on ahead. Mice, rabbits, and baby chipmunks were in cages that lined the open air market.

"But where are the birds?" Jo cried.

Marc pointed and Jo raced on. A minute later, Robin saw them. Splotches of yellow, blue, red, orange, purple, and green turned into birds of all colors chirping, moving restlessly around their wire cages, and gazing at the people staring at them.

"They're incredible!" cried Jo.

"Yes, they are very beautiful, are they not?" Mme Georges asked.

"I feel sorry for them locked up in their cages," Robin said quietly. No one else seemed to feel the same way. All around them, children were begging their parents to buy a bird, and men and women were inspecting the cages, looking for the perfect specimen. Other customers were there to purchase seed from men scooping the dried stuff out of huge burlap bags. An iron fountain, painted green, spurted water from the mouth of a statue, and children sat on the edge of its basin, splashing at each other. Robin watched, fascinated, as one of the bird sellers made his lunch. The man, wearing a blue jacket and faded blue cotton pants, wore a white cap pulled down on his forehead to shield him from the hot sun. Carefully, he sliced an onion with a big, sharp knife, then some dried sausage, and placed them neatly on one half of a long piece of French bread. He spread the other half with a thick brown paste and topped it with some sliced tomato. Then he wedded the two halves together and took an enormous bite.

Robin sniffed the pungent aroma of the onion, as well as the musty odor of birdseed.

"What was that he spread on his bread?" she asked Marc, in a low tone.

"*Pâté,*" he said. "It's made from liver. Delicious."

Robin started to make a face, but she was distracted by Jo.

"Look at me!" her sister cried. She sat on the curb with a brilliant green parakeet on her left shoulder and an orange one on her right. Sylvie snapped Jo's picture before the bird seller put the birds back, screeching and squawking, in their cages.

A white bird, a thick ruff of hair around its face, strutted by. Its owner watched it, but did not seem worried that it would get away.

"It can't fly," said Marc when Robin asked him about it. "I've seen this one before, but I don't know its name."

"Come!" said Mme Georges, clapping her hands. "We will have a quick lunch and then on to the flea market."

Nicolette welcomed them with ham and cheese sandwiches on long loaves of French bread, and green salad. A dish of yogurt and some fruit was dessert.

Jo made a face. "That's not dessert. That's health food. Yuk!"

Sylvie smiled. "In France, we eat fruit for dessert all the time. If it's fresh, it's so good." She peeled a peach for Jo and neatly quartered it, then topped it with some yogurt and a spoonful of sugar.

Jo took a bite and stopped complaining. "It's good," she said, and then added, "but not as good as chocolate ice cream."

Then the girls went upstairs to get ready. Jo went down the hall to the bathroom to wash up and comb her hair.

Robin decided to look at the picture again. She reached behind the sneakers, but she felt nothing. Robin took the sneakers out of the closet and searched more thoroughly. No picture. Where was it? Had someone broken in and stolen it?

Jo came whistling down the hallway. Robin grabbed her as she came through the door.

"Jo, something terrible has happened!"

"Are Mom and Dad okay?" Jo cried.

"Yes, nothing terrible like that," Robin said.

"Whew! You scared me," Jo said, sinking onto the bed. "What could be so terrible?"

"The package is gone. I can't find it," Robin said.

"Oh, no!" Jo cried. "Do you think someone stole it?"

"I don't know. We all went to the bird market today. No one was around the house except Nicolette," Robin said.

"I refuse to believe Nicolette took it," Jo said.

"You're just blinded by all those extra goodies she slips you," Robin said.

"Is it my fault if she likes me?" Jo replied. "It's a good thing she does give me extra food. Otherwise, I'd waste away on all this healthy stuff."

"Never mind the food," Robin said. "Help me empty out the closet again. Maybe it slipped behind something."

Suddenly, Jo looked sheepish. "Uh, Robin, uh, the package isn't missing."

"What? What do you mean?" Robin asked.

"I woke up last night and thought maybe the closet wasn't the best place to hide the picture. So I slipped it into my backpack under the bed," Jo admitted. "I'm sorry. I forgot to tell you." Sylvie knocked on their door.

"Jo, Robin. Are you ready? My aunt is waiting."

Without a word, Robin retrieved the backpack and handed it to Jo and they left the room.

Downstairs, Mme Georges tapped her foot.

"You girls are always late. What takes you so long?" she asked.

"My sister has a habit of losing things," Robin said as she walked out the door.

CHAPTER EIGHT

The Familiar Man

On the long ride to the flea market, Robin barely said a word to her sister. But once they got off, Jo turned to her and said, "You have to speak to me now."

"I can't believe you did that," Robin said.

"I said I was sorry. Now let's find out if this map is valuable," Jo said.

"All right," Robin said, grudgingly.

"Follow me," Mme Georges said. "If anyone gets lost, we will meet here in front of the métro station at five p.m." She pointed to a spot next to the station near a tiny restaurant.

Jo stared at the sign on the restaurant. "What a long name for such a tiny place," she said. "What does it mean?"

"It's an unusual name even for Paris," Marc said. "It means 'on the fourteenth of July there are always paper lanterns.'"

"No kidding," Jo said. "Really? You're not just making fun of me?"

"Really," said Marc. "You know that the fourteenth of July is Bastille Day in France, when we celebrate the storming of the prison in the days of the Revolution. There are always fireworks and parades and celebrations. You must have heard about it."

"I don't think so. I don't know anything about the Revolution," Jo said. "We haven't studied it yet in school."

"Then I will tell you about it," Marc said. "Or better yet, we'll go to the Conciergerie. Then you can see one of the places where some of the great events of the Revolution happened."

"Okay," said Jo. By now the group was threading its way through a narrow walkway lined with stalls. Jeans dangled from hangers, shoes, sunglasses, and watches were lined up neatly on tables, jewelry sparkled in the summer sun, and, farther on, the girls brushed against smooth black leather jackets hanging from hooks.

Women in long brown-and-green print dresses and turbans and boys in shorts and jeans strolled through, stopping to investigate tables filled with candy, wallets, or drums. A man thrust a soda can, sweating with cold, in Robin's face. "Five francs," he said, shaking the can at her.

Robin walked past, intent on her mission to find out more about the map. Jo hurried to catch up with her.

"Now we turn here, *mes amis,*" said Mme Georges. She led the group away from the crowds and through an arch. Robin saw her chance.

"Quick," she said to Jo. They ducked into the crowd and saw Mme Georges leading the group away.

"I don't think anyone saw us," Robin said. "Let's go this way."

She led Jo through an arch on the opposite side of the narrow passageway and into a little village of shops. Most of them displayed gleaming furniture, shining carved wooden desks, and big bureaus loaded on top with silver picture frames.

"I don't see anything that looks like maps," Jo said.

"Let's try to ask someone," Robin said.

Outside the shops, some antiques dealers had gathered to play cards, smoke cigarettes, and drink wine. They clustered around small card tables chattering and laughing.

Robin approached them and asked, "Excuse me, do you speak English?"

A man with a scraggly gray beard and thick gray eyebrows said, "Yes, a little. How can I help you?"

"We are looking for someone who knows something about maps," Robin said.

"Maps . . . I don't know. Do you know, Bernard?" The bearded man turned to one of his friends.

"Does everyone in Paris speak English?" Jo asked.

"We have to speak a little of everything. We have customers from all over the world. Perhaps you'd like to buy a table today?" he said and laughed.

"Uh, maps," Robin reminded him, patiently.

"How about Maître Pierre?" a woman asked.

All the dealers nodded. Maître Pierre, he would know. Yes, Maître Pierre for sure.

The bearded man pointed the way. "Through that courtyard and past the sign for the jewelry. You can't miss it."

"*Merci*," said Robin. "*Merci*," echoed Jo.

"Ah, you are learning French," said the man. "That is good. *Au revoir, mes petites.*"

Following the pathway leading to the courtyard, Robin and Jo sped past cases of necklaces and rings. Robin was tempted to stop but she didn't know how much time they would have before Mme Georges caught up with them.

Entering the courtyard from the dim passageway, they were dazzled by a brilliant burst of sunshine reflected from huge mirrors propped against the walls. Rugs in red, gold, and blue hung from a delicate black iron balcony, and huge jugs filled with tall grasses were ranged around the sides of the open space.

"I don't see anything about maps," Jo said.

"They said to go past the jewelry," Robin said.

"But we already did that," Jo said.

"Maybe there's another jeweler around here," Robin answered her.

The girls prowled the courtyard, looking. Just as they were about to give up, they saw a small white sign that said "Maître Pierre" in a tiny, dark alleyway. The door to the shop was closed.

"I don't see anyone in there," Jo said, as she peered through the glass in the doorway.

"Uh-oh," said Robin. Pulling her sister behind her, she ducked into a narrow niche beside the door.

Mme Georges was chattering in French as the group swept past in the courtyard. She seemed to be scolding Sylvie, who hung her head as she walked. Marc had his hand on Mme Georges's arm, but she shook him off. Sophie and Mario trailed at the back of the group, staring at the rugs.

"They must be looking for us," whispered Robin.

"And Mme Georges looks mad," Jo said. "We'd better have a good excuse when we meet them back at the train station."

"If they don't find us before then. I don't know how long we're going to have to wait for Maître Pierre," Robin said.

"I'm hungry," Jo said. "I can't wait that long. I have to eat something—otherwise I'm going to faint."

"We just had lunch," Robin muttered.

"There wasn't that much to eat," Jo said. "Listen. My stomach's rumbling."

"We have to find out about that map," Robin said. "I can't believe that it's not valuable. Jules seems so desperate to have it."

The girls settled themselves down on the ground in the alley and prepared to wait. Soon Jo dozed from boredom while Robin kept herself awake by making up stories about the map.

"Maybe it's to show where some treasure is buried," she thought. "Or maybe it's a very old map that is worth a lot of money."

She was embarking on another story when she heard footsteps coming their way.

"Wake up, Jo," she said.

Jo opened her eyes. "Where are we?" she asked. Then she realized and stood up with her sister.

"Someone's coming," Robin said.

A man with brown hair and eyeglasses seemed surprised to see them standing there.

"Maître Pierre?" Robin asked.

"*Oui,*" he said.

"Do you speak English?" she asked.

"*Oui,*" he said, then smiled. "Yes, I do."

"My sister and I have a map we want to show you and get your opinion on," Robin said.

Maître Pierre took out a large, thin key and opened the door to his shop. He ushered the girls inside. The walls were hung with maps and rolls of maps were piled high on top of tables.

Something black, flying through the air, screeched and landed on top of the maps. Robin jumped and Jo moved back.

"It is only my cat. She is mad with me because I left her for lunch. Come now, *chérie,* and I will give you some milk," said Maître Pierre.

He poured some milk in a saucer and stroked the cat.

Jo took the map out of her backpack and placed it on one of the tables.

"This is the map we want you to look at," said Robin.

Maître Pierre took the map up and peered at it closely. He took out a magnifying glass and looked over every inch of it. Then he put it down.

"Is it valuable?" Jo asked eagerly.

Maître Pierre shook his head slowly. "I am sorry to tell you this is just an ordinary, everyday map. Nothing special. You can buy them for five francs in any souvenir store. Did someone tell you it was worth a lot of money?"

"No, we just thought because Jules looked so . . ." Robin nudged Jo sharply, and the younger girl stopped talking.

"I am sorry," Maître Pierre repeated. "Can I help you with anything else?"

"No," said Jo.

"Yes," said Robin. "We'd like to get a present for our father. He collects old maps. Something not too expensive."

Maître Pierre's face lit up.

"I have here the very thing. It is old and very attractive. But you will have to have it framed. Do you want me to frame it for you? It will take a week."

"No, thank you," said Robin. "I think Dad will want to choose the frame himself."

"How much is it?" Jo asked.

"I will make a special fee for you," he said, naming a low price.

The girls waited while he rolled the map up carefully in tissue and brown paper and tied it with a string handle so Robin could carry it easily.

"Is Maître your first name?" Jo asked, while he was wrapping the map.

"No, it is Pierre," he said. "'Maître' means 'master' in French. They often call experts 'master.' And I am an expert on maps. *Voilà*," he said, handing Robin the package.

"Thank you very much," Robin said, and they left the tiny shop and walked out of the narrow alley.

"That was disappointing," Jo said.

"Yes," said Robin, "but at least now we know that we're not dragging anything valuable around."

"Why did you buy that map for Dad?" Jo asked. "He doesn't collect maps."

"Remember, I told Mme Georges that's why we wanted to come here. I have to show her something. Besides, it's a good excuse for getting lost. We can say we saw a map place, and ducked in thinking we could catch up with them. Then we lost them," Robin said.

"Always thinking," Jo said. "Now let's find something to eat."

"Always eating," Robin said. "Okay. I think there was ice cream and pizza back this way."

She turned to Jo to steer her in the right direction and saw her frowning as she studied a man walking past them.

"What's the matter?" Robin asked.

"I'm sure I know that man," Jo said. "He looks so familiar but I can't remember where I know him from."

"We haven't really met anyone in Paris, except the group at Mme Georges's," Robin said.

"No, and he wasn't a waiter at any of the restaurants," Jo said. "It'll come to me."

She looked puzzled as she walked on, but her face brightened as she came to the ice cream vendor.

"Look at all the flavors," she said to Robin.

Robin was impressed. There were varieties no one had back home: *poire* and *cassis* and *noisette*. From the pictures on the side of the stand she could guess that *poire* was pear and *cassis* was some kind of berry. But what was *noisette?*

She tried asking the vendor, who was a young girl. The girl giggled and made a crunching noise with her teeth. Crack! Crack!

"I don't get it," Jo said.

The girl put her hands up like paws and made funny faces. Then she showed Jo a scoop of the ice cream.

"Nuts! It's nuts!" Jo cried. "She was pretending to be a squirrel."

After that, Jo chose a cone of *noisette* ice cream, and Robin tried cassis.

"Pretty good," she said, licking it. "It sort of tastes like raspberry only sharper. I like the way they don't call them flavors here. They call them '*parfums*,' or perfumes."

They had passed through the arch again and now followed the path back to the market entrance and on to the métro station.

"Do you think Mme Georges will yell at us again?" Jo asked, a little fearfully.

"She's sure to," Robin said, licking her cone thoughtfully. "We'd better play it safe from now on, and not leave the group."

They crossed the huge street and passed a beggar sitting on the corner with a sign. Jo clutched Robin's arm.

"Robin, I know who that man is that we passed before. But he looks so different! I can't believe it!" she said.

"Who is it?" Robin asked.

"It's really strange," Jo said. "I don't understand it."

"Well, who is it?" Robin asked again. "Come on. Tell me."

"He's all cleaned up. He looks totally different. It's the radish man," Jo said.

CHAPTER NINE

The Radish Man Returns

 The girls were about to discuss the strange appearance of the radish man, when Sophie pounced on them.

"*Méchant!*" she cried, waving her finger at them.

"We're not merchants," said Jo. "We're just girls."

"She means that you have been very naughty," Sylvie said. "What's the matter? Don't you like being with us?"

"Of course we do," said Jo.

"But you do not act like it," Marc said. "You are always running away."

Mario looked at them reproachfully with big, sad eyes.

"We got lost," said Robin. "We saw this map store where I could buy my father a present. Then when we looked up, you were gone."

"Poor Mme Georges was very worried," Marc said.

"Where is she?" Jo asked, cringing.

"Aha!" Mme Georges appeared just then with a policeman in tow. She quickly explained something in French to the gendarme, who smiled, bowed, and walked away.

"I have been to the police to search for you girls. Where did you go?" She continued scolding them, her voice raised, as they walked through the métro station until the roar of the train drowned out her voice.

Robin noticed that Jo didn't seem as upset as before. In a low tone, she asked her sister, "Are you all right?"

Jo bounced along, smiling. "Yes. When Mme Georges screams, I've decided to pretend she's a parrot like the one we saw at the bird market. Squawk, squawk, squawk!"

Robin laughed and hugged her sister, while Mme Georges glared at them. She clamped a hand on each and shoved them into the métro car, then watched as they chose their seats. Mme Georges made sure to stand near them and to grab them when they rolled into the Odeon stop.

"Let us go," she said. "There will be no more losing. You will walk with me now."

Sylvie tried to intervene, but Mme Georges snapped at her and sent her back to walk with Sophie. The boys strolled ahead casually, but once Marc looked back and winked at Robin and Jo.

"Where are we going to dinner tonight, Madame?" Robin asked, politely.

"We are going to a bistro where the specialty is onion soup and liver," said Mme Georges. "But you two will be home with the good Nicolette. She will make you a meal. I am tired with trying to find you, tracking you down like those big dogs, how you say—ah, bloodhounds. You will stay in tonight. That is what happens to *jeunes filles* who do not stay with the group. Perhaps tomorrow you will be more happy to stay with us."

Robin and Jo tried to look downcast as they entered the house.

They trudged up to their room sorrowfully. Then they collapsed on the beds in giggles.

"She thinks she's punishing us by not making us eat liver!" shrieked Robin.

"Moldy old liver!" cried Jo.

"Shhh!" whispered Robin. "We don't want her to hear us." She put a pillow over Jo's head. Jo threw it back at her, and soon, in a fit of relief, the girls were having a pillow fight.

"Oof!" Robin had just heaved a pillow at Jo's stomach when they heard a polite knock at the door.

"Come in," Robin said, and tried to smooth her hair down. The pillows had landed on the floor and the bedspreads were half off the beds.

"*Tiens!* What has happened here?" Sylvie asked, looking shocked.

"We were having a pillow fight," Jo said, before Robin could shush her. "Didn't you ever have one?"

"Ah, no, my aunt would not permit it," Sylvie said. "I came to say I am sorry you will not be with us tonight. The bistro we are going to is most excellent."

"We're sorry too," said Robin, suppressing a smile. Jo just grinned behind her back.

"Nicolette will make anything you like," Sylvie said. "Perhaps I will see you when we return."

"Of course," said Robin, as Sylvie left the room slowly.

"Let's find out what Nicolette will make us," said Jo. "It's going to be fun having the whole house to ourselves."

"We'll clean up first and put away your backpack," Robin said.

"Why bother?" asked Jo. "We know the map's not worth anything."

"Still, Jules seems awfully anxious to get his hands on it," Robin said. "We'd better play it safe and hide it."

The girls took some time deciding where to hide the backpack. Finally, Robin crammed it behind some blankets on the top shelf of their closet.

"If anyone searches again, they will have already looked here," she said, tucking the straps of the backpack behind a gray wool blanket. "Now I'm ready."

"Take your French dictionary," Jo said. "Nicolette might not understand what we want."

The girls clambered downstairs to the breakfast room and looked for the housekeeper.

"Nicolette!" cried Jo. "Where are you?"

There was no answer. They peered into the tiny kitchen where Nicolette was to be found when she wasn't cleaning the house, but all they saw was a frying pan on the stove and some chopped onions on the counter.

"Nicolette?" Robin followed Jo to the tiny back entrance of the house. There they saw Nicolette handing some bread to a man wrapped in a blanket. He was sitting on the curb.

When Jo cried "Nicolette," the man looked up.

"It's the radish man!" Jo shouted, but the man scowled at the girls and turned his back. He muttered something to Nicolette, and waved her away. Nicolette walked towards the girls, her cheeks rosy with embarrassment.

"*Cet homme là n'est pas si gentil que cela,*" she said. She shook her fist in his direction, but the radish man, hunched over, gobbling his bread, never looked up.

"I guess he wasn't so nice to her," Robin said. Jo took Nicolette's hand and squeezed it.

"Never mind, Nicolette, we love you," Jo said.

Nicolette smiled and pinched Jo's cheek. Then the girls went into the house with her.

"What's for dinner?" Jo asked.

Nicolette looked blank, so Robin thumbed through her French-English dictionary.

"*Dîner?*" she asked.

"Ah," Nicolette nodded. She spouted a long stream of French that neither Jo nor Robin could understand.

Jo made a face and looked up at Nicolette questioningly. But Nicolette patted her and waved them off to the little sitting room.

The girls clicked on the TV, but there were only French programs. Jo went to turn it off, but Robin said, "Leave it on. It's good background noise in case anyone overhears us."

"But there's no one here except Nicolette, and she doesn't speak English," Jo said.

"We don't know that for sure," Robin said.

"Oh, come on," Jo said. "You have such a suspicious mind. You've read too many mysteries."

"Maybe," said Robin, "but somebody's after that map, and you, yourself, saw the radish man all cleaned up at the flea market. Now he's back here in rags. What do you think that means?"

"I wish I knew," Jo said.

"Think," Robin said.

"I can't on an empty stomach," Jo said. She sniffed the air. "I smell something good."

"Yes," said Robin, "it smells like meat."

"Good. You know what I'd like?" Jo asked dreamily. "I'd like a nice, thick hamburger and fries and a chocolate milk shake. I'm tired of experimenting with French food."

"Experimenting? We've hardly had anything different from what we eat at home," Robin scoffed.

"Nut ice cream? Yogurt? Fondue? You can't tell me we eat like this at home," Jo said.

"No, but they aren't very unusual things to eat," Robin said. "No one has made us eat snails or anything like that."

"Where's your French-English dictionary? I'm going to find out the French for hamburger and ask Nicolette," Jo said.

"*Dîner!*" Nicolette called.

The girls scrambled downstairs hungry for their dinner. Jo carried the little dictionary. Nicolette greeted them with a broad smile.

"*Dîner à la mode Américaine!*" she announced.

"What does that mean?" Jo whispered to Robin.

"'*À la mode*' means 'in the style of,'" Robin whispered back. "I think it means 'dinner, American style.'"

"*Voilà,*" Nicolette said as she brought in two plates filled with thick hamburgers and golden fries.

"How did she know?" Jo asked, as she bit into the juicy beef patty.

"I told you," whispered Robin. "Maybe she really does understand English."

Jo looked disbelieving, but tried to engage Nicolette in

conversation. The housekeeper simply shook her head, wiped her hands on her apron, and hurried back to the kitchen.

When the girls had finished their dinner, they brought their plates back to the tiny kitchen.

"Thank you, Nicolette. *Merci*," Robin said.

"*Merci*," echoed Jo.

Nicolette, her hands plunged into steaming, soapy water, beamed and nodded. Then her expression changed, and she tried to tell the girls something.

"*Soyez prudent*," she said, putting her finger to her lips.

"What do you mean, Nicolette?" Jo asked. "We don't understand French."

Nicolette repeated her words. Jo took out the French-English dictionary. Nicolette dried her hands on a dish towel, then took the dictionary from Jo and flipped through the pages. She pointed to a word.

Robin leaned over and read it. "'*Prudent*,'" she said. "It means 'prudent, careful, cautious.'"

"Are you saying you are careful?" Jo asked.

Nicolette frowned. "*Vous soyez prudent*," she repeated.

"You something careful," Robin translated. "You be careful? I think she's warning us."

"Be careful of what?" Jo asked.

Nicolette did not answer. She turned back to washing the dishes, as a breeze swept through the kitchen.

"There you are," Mme Georges said. "I hope Nicolette has given you an excellent meal, although you did not deserve it. We have had liver of such tenderness. It was unsurpassed. And delightful peach sorbet for dessert."

"We had hamburgers and french fries," Jo said, smiling. "I'd rather have that than liver any day."

"But you are a child and not a gourmet," Mme Georges replied. Then her expression changed. "Alas, I have sad news."

"What?" Robin asked.

"You remember that waiter, that Jules who served us the first night at Le Procope?" Mme Georges inquired, lifting an eyebrow.

Jo started to say "yes," but Robin poked her.

"Which one was he?" Robin asked. "Was he the tall one or the short one?"

"The one you spoke to at the race," Mme Georges said.

"That was someone else," Jo said, hotly.

"How would you know if you do not know who Jules is?" Mme Georges asked. "Never mind. You may play your games. Poor Jules had an accident. He is in the hospital. I fear he is gravely ill."

The tiny kitchen felt crowded to Robin. She tried to leave, but Mme Georges blocked their way. She pushed back her blonde hair and continued, "He was walking down the street yesterday, so innocently. Then he crossed the street and a car hit him. We do not know if he will survive. I am a very good friend of his. Any messages you have for him, you can give to me."

She waited expectantly, glancing from Jo to Robin.

"We have no messages for him," Robin said. "We barely know the man."

"Ah, it is good to be careful. Wasn't that what Nicolette was telling you before? I must speak to her, and see why she said that. One would think she knows something," Mme Georges said, tapping her teeth with her long, pink fingernail.

"Excuse me, Madame, we would like to go to our room," Robin said. "My sister and I are tired."

"By all means," said Mme Georges. "Think about poor Jules, lying there, perhaps never to see his mother again. I believe she is old and lives in the mountains. Well, we shall see. Death must come to all."

"By the way," said Robin, summoning up her courage, "what hospital is this waiter in?"

"What hospital?" Mme Georges raised her eyebrows. "Why do you want to know?"

"You said he was in a hospital. Which one?" Robin persisted.

Mme Georges smiled as if something amused her. "He is at Les Soeurs de Sainte Thérèse. But he is permitted no visitors. *Alors,* you must get some rest. Tomorrow we go to the Museum of Magic and Curiosity. You will enjoy it. You will see many things you will not be able to explain there."

Fooling the Eye

The next day the group set off early in the morning. Mme Georges had elected not to go with them.

"She is in a bad mood," Sylvie said. "One of her friends is sick. I am pleased to be going since I have never been to this museum."

Robin tried not to look too knowing. "Where is this museum?" she asked.

"It's in the Marais," Sylvie said. "It's a very old district with many small antiques shops and cobblestone streets."

"Is anything new in Paris?" Jo asked.

"Yes, there is a new area called La Défense, where there are skyscrapers," Sylvie said. She paused. "Of course, everyone thinks it is ugly," she admitted.

As the group walked one by one on the narrow sidewalks, Robin admired the sparkling jewelry in the windows. Now and then she saw a courtyard opening off the street, and could peer through and see more little shops, and once an art exhibit.

Finally, they crossed the street in front of a tiny café with one table and two chairs outside. There, facing them, was a building with a red door and a black sign painted to look like a curtain. The sign said: "*Académie de Magie.*"

A giant toy dispenser painted with a woman's face and a design of playing cards stood guard at the entrance. Jo and Robin followed the others down narrow, steep steps to the basement, where a poster on the wall showed the "World's Greatest Magician," a man with a mustache wearing an orange turban with a white feather.

"Shake hands with the magician," Marc said, and laughed at Robin's expression when she shook the hands of a dummy, who raised and lowered his arm and tipped his hat.

"Look!" Jo shrieked. A painting on the wall collapsed as they watched.

An unsmiling young man with dark hair and a thin, wispy mustache took their tickets. Jo tried to ask him questions, but he only spoke French.

"I will translate for you, Jo," Sylvie said. She spoke with the young man for a few minutes, then turned to Jo.

"There are many illusions here. Some are what they call *trompe l'oeil* or 'fool the eye.' They may look like one thing but are actually another. There is also a magic show later," she said.

As they entered a dark corridor, Jo clutched Robin's hand. They could hear faint shrieks in the distance, and a roaring kind of noise.

"Don't worry," Robin whispered. "I'm sure there's nothing to be afraid of."

They emerged into a large room with better lighting filled with cases of magician's paraphernalia. Robin inspected a case of wands, while Jo looked at some trick cards.

"Not very interesting," she said, as she drifted over to Robin.

"Jo, come here," Marc said. He led her and Sophie to a small room where there were big cases with lions' heads on them.

"Put your hands here," he instructed and showed her where to put her hands in the opening that formed the lion's mouth.

"What's supposed to happen now?" Jo asked, and just then a mighty roar from the lion's mouth made her jump.

Sophie and Marc giggled, and Jo tried to catch them, but Marc eluded her. She scooped up Sophie and tickled the little ten year old. "That's for fooling me," she said, smiling.

Jo and Sophie tried out all the different lion-head games. Most of the time the lion roared, but once Jo was startled when a piece of leather flicked at her fingers. It was supposed to be the lion's tongue.

They amused themselves with the funhouse mirrors, going from tall Jo and Sophie to short and fat Sophie and Jo. Then they spied Robin and Sylvie, who were studying a box containing green dice.

Jo tried to scoop them up, but her fingers fumbled on the smoothness of the case.

"It looks like you can pick them up," she complained.

"Ah, remember I told you about fool the eye," said Sylvie. She pointed to a box mounted on the wall. If you looked at it one way, it looked flat, the other way, three dimensional.

Robin walked past Marc and Mario, and Marc told her to wait with them. They were staring at a picture on the wall. After a few minutes, a ghost appeared in the painting, then disappeared.

"This is really a cool place," Robin said. Marc started to answer her, but a man with white hair and a salt-and-pepper-colored suit stepped into the middle of the room and started to lecture. Jo and Robin stood politely as the man spoke in French for at least fifteen minutes. Finally, he stopped and bowed, and everyone clapped.

"What did he say?" Robin asked Marc.

"He said that the museum has been here for a while, and he talked about the history of magic. Then he said the magic show is about to start. Let's get seats."

Marc led the way back to the dark corridor, where bleacher-style seats had been screened off to create a small theater. The girls scrambled up to the top; the boys sat one row below them.

A young man in a black suit came out and started by bowing and welcoming everyone in French.

"We're not going to understand a word," hissed Jo.

"Shh! Give it a chance," Robin said. "Anyway, we're trapped here. There's nowhere to go."

Jo measured the drop to the floor from the height of the bleachers and settled back in her seat. Robin was right; there was no way out. She moved closer to Robin, who was seated at the end of their row.

"Watch out!" Robin whispered. "You almost pushed me over the edge."

Soon, however, the girls became absorbed in the show. Even though the magician spoke French throughout, the girls could guess what he was saying as they saw what he was doing.

First, he held up three pieces of string. Each one was a different length. Then he squeezed them together in the palm of his hand. He revealed that they had turned into one long string. Then he crushed them in his palm again, waved his hand three times, and took out three pieces of string, all the same length. Finally, he waved his hand again and took out the pieces of string one by one. Now they were all different lengths again.

More tricks followed with cards and balls. Robin was watching a trick where the magician made balls of different colors appear when she felt something thrown into her lap. She could feel it was a piece of paper, but it was so dark she couldn't see anything. The paper crackled as she slid it into her pocket.

When the magician took his final bow, everyone applauded and the lights came on. Robin and Jo jumped down the steps and rejoined Sophie and Sylvie at the entrance to the makeshift theater.

Robin started to slide the paper out of her pocket, but Sylvie was rounding everyone up. Then the group was on the move again, climbing up the stairs and out into the street.

"Nicolette has the day off today," Sylvie said, "so we will eat lunch at a café. There is a good one at the Place des Vosges."

They traipsed down a few narrow streets and turned into a main street. They kept on walking until Robin thought she would scream. All she wanted was to stop some place and read the paper that she had hidden in her pocket.

Suddenly, they turned left and walked through a large stone arch. Stone walls surrounded them. Robin couldn't imagine where the café was. Then they stepped through another arch into a large square. There was a park filled with leafy trees in the middle, and cafés all around at the edges of the square.

"Pizza!" cried Jo, spying a café that advertised it. She hopped from foot to foot until they settled themselves at a long table under an arcade.

A waiter came dashing up and Sylvie ordered pizza and drinks for all of them. Robin chewed her pizza automatically and thought about how she could read the note as soon as possible.

"Where are we going next?" she asked Sylvie, hoping it was back to the house.

Marc smiled wickedly. "To the Conciergerie, where you will see what happens to people who lose their heads."

Sylvie laughed. "Marc is being very dramatic, but it is an interesting place, and quite near to our house. So we will have a short walk back home."

Sophie and Jo wanted lemon ices. Robin tapped her foot impatiently. Then she had an idea.

"I must find the rest room," she said. "I'm greasy from that pizza. I want to wash up."

"I will go with you," Sylvie said. "I, too, want to freshen up. Come, Sophie, I will take you, also."

"I'm fine," said Jo. "I'll stay with the boys."

Robin went off with the others. Now her plan was spoiled. She wouldn't be alone to look at the paper, and she did not want to share it with anyone yet. Perhaps Jules had written her a note? But how could that be? He was in the hospital, wasn't he? Who else could it be? Robin resolved to look at the paper as soon as she could.

In the ladies' room, Sylvie washed her hands and Sophie's. "Excuse me," murmured Robin as she entered one of the stalls. She waited a minute, then flushed the toilet to cover up any noise as she took out the paper.

There, written in big, black letters, was a message: "GIVE IT UP AND LEAVE IT ON TOP OF THE BUREAU IN YOUR ROOM." Robin crumpled the paper in her fist, then crammed it into her pocket. What did it mean? She came out of the stall and washed her hands.

Sylvie was combing Sophie's hair.

"I'm ready," said Robin, washing her hands. "Let's go."

When they came out, the boys were waiting.

"You look very serious, Robin," Marc said. "Is anything the matter?"

"No, everything's fine," said Robin, forcing herself to smile.

"Paris can be a strange place. You must be very careful," Marc said, and glided away to steer Mario in the right direction.

As they walked to the métro, Robin turned to Sylvie and asked, "Would it be possible for you to show me and my sister where something is when we get back to the house?"

"Certainly," Sylvie said. "What are you looking for?"

"We have a friend here who is in the hospital," said Robin. "We would like to visit, if possible."

"I would be happy to go with you," Sylvie said. "Which hospital is it?"

"The Soeurs de Sainte Thérèse," Robin said.

"Oh, yes, that is quite near to the house," Sylvie said. "What happened to your friend? Is it an illness or an accident?"

"I'm not sure," Robin said. "My mother told me to look this person up, and I called and found out he was in the hospital."

"It is not a problem," Sylvie said. "I will tell Aunt Amélie and we will go tomorrow."

"Do you think we could go after the Conciergerie, and before we go back to the house?" Robin asked.

"Yes, it is possible. It is on our way. But we may be late for dinner then," Sylvie replied.

"We won't stay long. I just want to make sure he's all right. There's no need to tell your aunt about it," Robin said.

"There is nothing wrong with this, is there?" Sylvie asked. Clearly, she was worried about not telling her aunt.

"Oh, no, but your aunt is inclined to fuss when we do things on the spur of the moment," Robin said.

"'Spur of the moment,'" Sylvie said, wrinkling her brow. "I do not understand this."

"Spontaneously. By chance. Not always according to the plan," Robin said, trying desperately to translate the meaning.

"Ah! Now I understand," Sylvie said, nodding. "But this is a serious responsibility, taking care of other people's children. You see. It is not something to be done lightly. Aunt Amélie is always telling me that."

"That's true. But you don't tell your aunt everything, do you?" Robin asked.

Sylvie blushed and shook her head.

"Bingo!" Robin thought to herself. "So please don't tell her about the hospital visit. Okay?" she asked Sylvie.

Slowly Sylvie nodded. "Okay," she said.

"What are you two gabbing about?" Jo said, walking backwards to fall in with them.

"Nothing much," Robin said. "Did you like the museum?"

"It was so cool," Jo said. "When we get back home, I'm going to learn some magic tricks."

"Why don't you turn around and walk the regular way first?" Robin suggested.

"It's more fun to walk this way," Jo said. "Besides, this way I get to see Paris in a different way—backwards. I don't know many people who can say that, do you Sylvie?"

"No, I think you are the only one to hold that distinction," Sylvie said, smiling.

Just then they reached the curb and before Robin could warn her, Jo tripped. Marc sprang towards Jo quickly, and caught her before she could fall.

"I told you to be careful in Paris," he said, looking at Robin. "This can be a very dangerous city."

CHAPTER ELEVEN

Lost and Found

All through their visit to the Conciergerie, Robin was lost in thought. She passed through the huge Salle des Gend'Armes without noticing the high, vaulted ceilings. She barely glanced at the plaque of a woman's head with a snake emerging from it.

Jo was entranced with the small room showing a model of the clerk of the court. The man wore a black tricorn hat, a white shirt, and a black vest and was ready to mark down the names of the prisoners with a big quill pen and a large book with lined pages. Mario stared at the concierge, or keeper of the prison, in his room.

"I would have liked to have been the concierge of the prison," Jo said to Sylvie. "It must have been great to order all the food and be in charge of the supplies."

"Not so wonderful all the time," Sylvie answered. "Sometimes the concierge was charged with stealing, and he was sentenced to death."

"It all depends on the way you look at it," murmured Robin.

"What?" asked Marc. "Did you say something, Robin?"

Robin jumped. "Nothing," she said. "I just . . ."

"I want to see Marie Antoinette's room," Jo cried. "Let's go there next."

She raced down the steps to it, almost colliding with a group that was coming up. Jo stopped before Marie Antoinette's room when she came to a video that described the French Revolution. It told about the people's desire for democracy and the famous people who had been killed.

Robin peered into Marie Antoinette's room and saw the figure representing the tragic queen. The mannequin, her head covered by a black shawl, was placed with her head turned away from the viewer. Standing behind her, in back of a screen, loomed a tall soldier dressed in a red, white, and blue uniform.

"Let's go see where the privileged prisoners stayed," Marc suggested. They climbed a narrow staircase and found a cell where a wax figure of a man sat on a chair reading a book by lantern light.

"Humph! That doesn't look so privileged to me," Jo said.

"Oh, that cell was the best. It was for the rich and famous," Marc said. "Here's where the privileged stayed." He pointed to a cell where two male figures sat, each on a cot. Between them, two wooden bowls rested on a chair.

"They were lucky," Sylvie said. "They had beds."

Finally, the group reached the Straw Quarters, where hundreds of prisoners had slept on straw spread on the floor.

"I can't imagine how awful that must have been," Jo remarked, as Mario shivered in sympathy.

The group ended their tour by passing through a doorway with a water trough beside it into a little courtyard where a brown fence enclosed four trees and a small patch of grass.

"It was here that the women prisoners washed their clothes," Marc said. "Sometimes they were able to chat with the men, although that was forbidden."

"Poor, poor people," Jo said, "waiting for their heads to be cut off." She shuddered despite the warm sunshine pouring down into the clearing.

"Come, this is too nice a day to be thinking about tragedies," Sylvie said. "We will get an ice cream now."

In a rapid change of mood, Jo grabbed Sophie's hand and raced to the exit. Robin and Sylvie walked behind the boys, and Robin said, "You haven't forgotten about visiting the hospital, have you?"

"Of course not," said Sylvie. "We will go after we get our ice cream."

Licking their cones, the group walked home slowly. When they came to the left turn for the house, Sylvie said to the boys, "Please take Sophie back with you."

"Where are you going?" Marc asked.

"I've asked Sylvie to take us to buy a few things we need," Robin said.

A knowing look came over Marc's face. "Girl things, I guess," he said.

"That's right," Robin said, grinning. "You'd be bored."

"All right. Come on, Sophie. You're not really a girl yet." He and Mario picked up the little girl and swung her back and forth as they walked away. Sophie's giggles followed Robin, Jo, and Sylvie as they made their way to the hospital.

"Where are we going?" Jo asked.

"We're going to visit Mom and Dad's friend in the hospital," Robin said.

"What friend?" Jo asked, looking puzzled.

Robin kicked her. "You know, their friend from that restaurant back home."

"Oh, that friend!" exclaimed Jo, rubbing her ankle. "Why didn't you tell me?"

"I forgot. Sylvie will show us the way," Robin said.

Eventually, they turned into a broad street and Sylvie took them to a gray stone building. The entrance was flanked by two stone carvings of angels. Etched over the door was the name "Les Soeurs de Sainte Thérèse."

Sylvie started to climb the steps with them, but Robin said, "It's best if we go alone. Our parents' friend is very shy, and hates to meet strangers."

"But how will you make yourself understood? You do not speak French. How will you find the room?" Sylvie asked.

"We have to do something ourselves," Robin said, her eyes flashing. "We're not babies! Can't you just leave us alone?"

Sylvie pressed her lips together. "Very well. I will wait out here. If you need me, you know where to find me."

"That wasn't too nice," Jo said to Robin as they went into the hospital.

"I know, but I couldn't have her hanging around when we asked for Jules," Robin said. "We don't even know what his last name is."

They tiptoed down a long, dimly lit hallway lined with statues. Frequently, nuns brushed past them, dressed in black-and-white habits that rustled as they moved. Finally, they reached a gray-haired woman in a black suit sitting at a desk.

"Pardon me," said Robin, "do you speak English?"

"Yes, my child. What is it?" the woman responded.

"We want to see one of your patients," Jo said.

"The name?" the woman asked, poised over a big ledger.

"His first name is Jules. We don't know his last name," Robin said.

"When was he admitted?" the woman asked.

"Two days ago," Jo said.

The woman turned the thick pages of the book. Then she looked up and shook her head.

"I am sorry. There was no one with the Christian name of Jules admitted two days ago. Perhaps he is at a different hospital."

"Could you look again?" Robin asked.

The woman ruffled the pages. "I have looked through the entire past two weeks. No patient named Jules has been here."

"Thank you," Robin said, and the girls walked away.

"What does it mean?" Jo asked. "Mme Georges said Jules was here. Where is he?"

"I don't know, but I think it's extremely important that we get to our room now, and that we go to Notre-Dame tomorrow," Robin said.

"Why our room?" Jo asked.

"Something occurred to me after we visited the museum. If I'm right, we've been looking at why this package is so important all along. But we just didn't see it."

"I wish you wouldn't be so mysterious," Jo grumbled.

"Never mind. And don't say anything to Sylvie," Robin said.

"What do we tell her about the sick friend?" Jo asked.

"I'll think of something," Robin said.

They walked down the thick stone steps to see Sylvie patiently sitting on a bench, waiting for them.

"So, what happened? That was a quick visit. Was your friend glad to see you?" Sylvie asked, rising to join them.

"She had checked out already," Robin said. "I guess she's gone back to the U.S."

"I thought your friend was a man," Sylvie said, accusingly.

"No, it was a woman, Mrs. Sheffield is her name," Robin said. "I never said it was a man."

"I must have been mistaken," Sylvie said, and she walked on, chatting pleasantly with the girls.

At the corner, Jo said, "The radish man is gone again."

"Who?" asked Sylvie.

Robin and Jo explained the name to her.

"There are many of these men around. They are ruined for good by alcohol," she said. "They come, they go. Who knows what happens to them?"

When they reached the house, they found the boys and Sophie in the sitting room.

"Come on," Marc said. "We've been waiting for you. We're ready to play Monopoly."

"I want to go upstairs first," Robin said. "Jo wants to go too."

"You spend so much time in your room," Marc complained. "You must have something important hidden there."

"There's nothing at all!" exclaimed Jo. "We just need to wash up."

"Okay, okay. Calm down. We'll wait for you," Marc said. "But hurry it up."

Robin and Jo ran up the stairs. As soon as they got into the room, Robin retrieved the backpack from its hiding place and took the package out. She tore off the brown paper wrapping and looked at the map again. Then she turned the frame over and undid the clasps on the back.

"What are you doing?" Jo asked.

"If I'm right, this will explain everything," Robin said. She removed the stiff backing, and shook the map loose from its frame. Then she turned it over. The map fell away and there, staring up at the girls, was a young girl in a white dress, with a white fur stole thrown over her shoulders.

"What is that?" Jo gasped.

"It's the painting that Marc told us about. The one that was stolen from the *château* in the Loire Valley."

"Hurry and hide it," Jo said. "We'll have to talk about this later."

The girls bundled the painting up in the map again and wrestled with the stiff clasps until they got the two back in the picture frame. Jo clasped the backpack to her.

"I don't know where to put this anymore," she said.

"We'll put it back where we hid it," Robin said. "Obviously, it's still safe here."

"What made you think it was behind the map?" Jo asked.

"It was all that stuff about fooling the eye," Robin said. "Then you started me thinking when you talked about seeing Paris in a different way—by walking backwards."

"I never would have thought of it," Jo said, admiringly.

"Now we have to figure out how to get it to the police," Robin said. "We don't want to be responsible for this a minute longer than we have to."

"Can we ask someone to help us?"

"I don't know if we can trust anyone," Robin said.

Jo shivered. "That sounds terrible. It sounds like we're trapped with a bunch of thieves."

"We definitely can't trust Mme Georges," said Robin.

"Agreed," said Jo.

"And we can't communicate with Mario," Robin continued.

"Sophie's a baby," said Jo, scornfully.

"And Sylvie's too much under her aunt's influence," said Robin.

Jo brightened. "What about Marc?"

Robin answered slowly. "I'm really not sure, and we can't take the chance."

"Then we're in this all alone," Jo said. "That's creepy. The only thing that makes me feel better is that no one knows we have it."

"That's right. No one knows. Now let's go play Monopoly, and we'll figure something out later," Robin said. She let Jo go out of the room first.

"I'll be down in one second," she said to her sister, ducking back into the room. Then she took the threatening note out of her pocket, tore it into little pieces, and threw it in the wastebasket.

"Robin?" she heard her sister call.

"Coming," she answered, and slammed the door of the room.

"Is everything okay?" Jo asked anxiously, as they walked down the stairs.

"Everything's fine, just fine," Robin answered.

A Fashion Victim

 That night, the girls agreed. They would take the painting to the police the next day.

"It's too valuable to leave lying around," Robin said. "But we'll go to Notre-Dame and try to find Jules."

"After we've given the painting to the police," Jo said.

"Absolutely. We'll sneak out of the house early in the morning and go to the police station," Robin said.

The next morning, the girls woke before it was fully light and dressed hurriedly. Robin took the backpack out and slid her arms through the straps.

"We'll tiptoe out," she said.

"What if Mme Georges finds out we're gone?" Jo asked.

"We'll let the police explain it to her," Robin said.

They crept down the stairs in the dark. Robin didn't dare to turn on any lights. They reached the front door without making a sound. No one seemed to be up, not even Nicolette, who was an early riser.

Robin reached out to grasp the front door knob when a sharp voice rang out: "*Bonjour!*"

The girls turned to see Mme Georges descending the staircase. "I see you are up early. Very good. You can help Nicolette with the breakfast. Come now." She grabbed each of their wrists with her strong hands and dragged them downstairs to the kitchen.

"Nicolette! Nicolette!" The housekeeper slowly walked into the kitchen, rubbing the sleep out of her eyes.

In rapid French, Mme Georges spoke to Nicolette and pointed to the girls. Then she floated out of the kitchen, casting a backwards glance at the girls. Soon, Nicolette had them squeezing oranges for juice while she ground coffee beans. Under cover of the noise, Robin whispered to Jo, "As soon as we're done, let's slip out. Mme Georges can't watch us all the time."

But Sylvie entered the kitchen, and helped them carry the food to the table, where Sophie sat waiting. She clearly expected the girls to sit with her at breakfast, so Robin and Jo found themselves unwillingly chewing croissants and sipping hot chocolate with the older girl and the ten year old.

Soon Mario and Marc came in, yawning. Mario smiled and said "*bonjour*" to the girls, but Marc simply grabbed the orange juice and drank it as fast as he could. Then he bowed and said, "Ladies."

"And where are we going today?" he asked, as Mme Georges entered the room.

"Notre-Dame," Mme Georges said, casting a sharp glance at Robin. She walked over to her, and put her hand on Robin's shoulder.

"You do not need to wear this at breakfast," she said. "I do not understand these American fashions. Those ugly shoes instead of something chic. These loads you carry. You will end up looking like a little camel with, how you call it, ah yes, a lump on your back."

Jo giggled in spite of herself. "You mean a hump, Madame."

"Hump, lump, you must take this off before you develop one," Mme Georges said.

"I'm fine, really, Madame," Robin said, twitching the straps of the backpack securely onto her shoulders.

"Really, it's cool back home to have a lump," Jo continued, through her giggles. "Only the nerds don't have them."

"*Bien,* Madame, we must leave them to their fads," Marc said, lazily.

Mme Georges shrugged, picked up her cup of coffee, and sipped in silence. Occasionally, she admired her feet in their usual open-toed high heels.

"What a good idea to go to Notre-Dame," Sylvie said, trying to make up for her aunt's curtness.

Robin shivered. She much preferred to go to the police station before they saw Jules, but she didn't know how to go about it.

"Come. Let us go." Mme Georges got up from the table and took Jo's hand.

Robin saw her sister shrink from Mme Georges's touch.

"Do we take the métro, Madame?" she asked, to distract the older woman.

"No, it is but a short walk from here. Come, Jo, you will walk with me, and tell me your impressions of Paris." Mme Georges escorted Jo neatly out the door and up the stairs. Robin ran to catch up.

"I will walk with you, Madame," she said.

"There is not enough space here," Mme Georges said, indicating the narrow sidewalk. "Walk with Sylvie, please."

Robin fell back by Sylvie's side, and tried to pay attention to Sylvie's chatter. What was Mme Georges up to now?

When they came to the great plaza in front of the cathedral, Mme Georges glanced at her watch. It was nine-thirty.

"Good. The crypt has just opened," she announced. She led the group down stone steps and into a dark room.

"Where are we going?" Robin asked.

"It's part of Paris's past," Marc answered. "Three hundred years B.C., there was a tribe of fishermen, hunters, and boatmen who settled here. They were called the Parisii. And that's where we get the name Paris. This crypt shows some of the earliest foundations of Paris, and some items they found that later people used."

Robin strolled around the dimly lit museum, staring at ancient rocky walls and deep pits in the earth. All the while, she was trying to keep track of Jo and Mme Georges. She patted the backpack reassuringly. The least she could do was keep the picture safe until they got it to the police.

From time to time, she caught sight of Mme Georges and Jo. The woman seemed to be lecturing her sister, and Robin ran to catch up with them. But someone stepped in her way.

Robin gasped in horror as the man stumbled in front of her. He kept mumbling something in French. Robin tried to dodge him, but he kept getting in her way. Finally, she shoved him and the man gave way. He muttered something again, and drifted off. But now, to her horror, Robin saw that the whole group had left the crypt.

Robin ran up the stairs and outside. Where was her sister? In the distance, she saw the group walking but there was no sign of Mme Georges or Jo. She raced to catch up with the rest.

Sylvie turned around as Robin gasped, "Where's Jo?"

"Isn't she with you? Actually, we thought you had all gone ahead."

Sylvie patted Sophie's blonde head and spoke to her in French, then turned and translated for Robin.

"I told her we must be quiet and respectful in the cathedral. The priest gets very annoyed with the tourists. You may hear him."

"Is your aunt in the cathedral?" Robin asked.

"I believe so. Did you see her go in, Marc?" Sylvie asked.

"Yes, and Jo was with her. So you do not have to worry, Robin," he said reassuringly.

Robin hurried past the others towards the cathedral. If she had not been so worried, she would have admired the pale cream color of the church, and the delicate, lace-like appearance of its towers. Instead, she jumped as she noticed the leer of one of the gargoyles leaning down from the right side.

As Robin entered the dimness of Notre-Dame, she automatically looked up to the great vaulted ceilings. Behind the altar, one of the famous rose windows glowed, its blue, red, and green stained glass formed in the shape of the flower. Candle lights flickered on either side, and dark niches invited private prayers in various sections.

"I don't see Jo," Robin said.

"Perhaps she is over there lighting a candle," Sylvie said. "I often light one when I come here. It is only ten francs."

She showed Robin the row of candles and the sign that said, "The candle is a witness to your prayer; it will burn after you have gone."

"Come, light your candle and then we will climb to the bell tower," Sylvie said.

Robin ignored the candles and scanned the vast cathedral. Wooden chairs were set up for worshippers. The enormous space made everyone look tiny. Robin started to walk around, peering intently, trying to find Jo in the dim light.

As she passed one of the dark niches, Robin heard a whisper: "Robin, in here." There she saw Jo huddling in a corner, pressed close to a saint carved in stone.

"What's going on?" Robin asked in her normal voice.

"You will give up the painting now," said Mme Georges, from the darkness, "or your sister will pay the price."

"Jo, are you okay?" Robin asked, disregarding the threatening woman.

"She made me whisper to you," whimpered Jo. "She's twisting my arm. She threatened to hurt me if you don't give her the painting."

"What makes you think I have the painting?" Robin asked.

The older woman gave a short, harsh laugh.

"You must think I am a fool. Jules told me, of course," she said. "I had my suspicions, but he confirmed them."

"Where was Jules? We went to the hospital and he wasn't there," Robin said.

"He was safe in another hospital. He won't try to, how do you Americans say it, cross me again," Mme Georges said.

"You mean double cross," Jo said scornfully. Then she yelped as Mme Georges twisted her arm again.

"Whatever you call it, we have a very nice little enterprise going. Jules and his friends steal the paintings, and I sell them. But Jules became greedy and wanted the money all for himself. That was a big error," Mme Georges boasted.

"So it was you who dropped the note in my lap when we were at the magic show," Robin said.

"Who else? If you had given the painting up, we would not have had to go through this comedy," Mme Georges said. "Now I grow weary of this. Let us finish our business here."

Robin peered through the darkness, trying to see if Mme Georges had a weapon. She thought the woman had nothing in her hands, but she couldn't take the chance. Not when she was holding Jo.

"Do you have a gun or a knife?" she asked.

Mme Georges laughed scornfully. "You Americans are so violent. Of course not. I simply have very strong hands. Your sister's little arm will snap if I twist it the right way."

Just then the loudspeaker boomed. Robin was startled to hear a voice say in English: "Notre-Dame is not a museum. It is a living house of worship. If you want to attend mass, the next service will be in ten minutes. If not, we ask you to depart quietly without disturbance. If you attend the service, perhaps this will make your visit more meaningful than that of the usual tourist attraction."

Robin looked around desperately. If only she could attract someone's attention.

"We are quite alone here," Mme Georges purred. "Now, you will hand over that package."

"Let go of my sister first," Robin said. Her body was shaking but she gritted her teeth.

"Very well," said Mme Georges. "But you must come close to me."

Jo skittered away from Mme Georges and pressed close to Robin.

"Do not think of yelling," Mme Georges said. "They get very angry about any interruptions here. You will be thrown out and I will explain in French. No one will believe you."

"Stand back, Jo," Robin said. Her hands were trembling.

She moved closer to Mme Georges. Robin could smell the sickeningly sweet perfume Mme Georges was wearing.

For a second, Robin closed her eyes, mentally reviewing Mme Georges, thinking about any weak spots she might have seen on the older woman. Then she dropped the backpack at Mme Georges's feet.

"*Bien*. You are a sensible girl." Mme Georges bent over the backpack to pick it up, and Robin slammed her foot down on Mme Georges's bare toes as hard as she could.

"Ow!" Mme Georges screamed, and Robin swiftly followed up by reaching down and grasping the woman's ankle. Mme Georges collapsed in a heap, and Robin picked up the backpack and yelled "Run!" to Jo.

The girls raced out of the niche with Mme Georges limping as quickly as she could behind them. "*Voleuses!*" she shouted.

Jo and Robin sped out of the main area of the cathedral only to barrel into a priest. He began scolding them in French, and Mme Georges came hobbling up.

"*Voleuses! Voleuses!*" she said, panting. She pointed at the backpack.

The priest scowled at Jo and Robin, then patted Mme Georges gently on the arm. They began a lengthy conversation in French.

"What are they saying?" Jo was still trembling from her encounter with Mme Georges.

"I don't know, but it looks like she's accusing us of something," Robin responded. "I wish Sylvie or Marc were here to translate."

"Where are they?" Jo asked.

"In the bell tower," Robin said. The priest looked threateningly at Robin.

"Quick! Let's get out of here," Robin said. The priest tried to catch her, but Robin was too fast for him. Jo and Robin ran through the crowds, as people stopped and stared. Mme Georges and the priest chased them, both now yelling "*Voleuses!*"

They were almost at the front steps and out the massive entrance when two hands reached out and grabbed Robin and Jo. They tried to wiggle free but the hands clamped on their arms and held them firmly.

"You must stop now," the voice said in French-accented English. "All will be well."

Jo looked up and a bewildered expression crossed her face.

"Robin, it's the radish man," she said.

"Please give me your sack," the radish man said. He was now dressed neatly in a clean navy jacket and brown pants. His brown hair was carefully combed, and he looked as if he had just shaved. The radish man's blue eyes twinkled as both Robin and Jo stared at him.

"I'm only giving the backpack to the police," Robin said. "It contains something valuable that was stolen."

"How well I know," the radish man said. He took a badge out of jacket pocket and showed it to Robin.

"What's that?" she asked.

"I am with the French police. I am Inspector Bernard," he said.

"But . . . but . . . you begged on the street corner," Jo said. "I even gave you money."

"*Merci*," said Inspector Bernard. "You have heard of the under the cover kind of policeman?"

"Under the cover? Oh, you mean an undercover cop," Robin said.

"Yes, I have been watching Mme Georges's house for some time now. We got a tip from one of Jules's pals and found out that Mme Georges was the brains behind the thefts from the *châteaux*."

"How did you know we had the painting?" Robin asked.

"I wasn't sure until Mme Georges visited Jules in the hospital to threaten him. He told her who had the painting. I pretended to be a hospital worker and listened in on the conversation. After that, we followed her and watched. My superiors wanted to make sure she did not damage the painting before we recovered it," Inspector Bernard said. He held out his hand for the painting.

"How do I know for sure you're with the police," said Robin, "and not part of Mme Georges's gang?"

"My colleagues have arrested her," the inspector said. "You see!" He waved to two men who were dragging Mme Georges out of the cathedral. They waved back and Mme Georges shot a glance full of hate towards Robin and Jo, and then she was gone from sight.

Robin handed the painting to the inspector, who unwrapped it. Sylvie came running up with Marc, Mario, and Sophie behind her.

"What has happened, Robin?" she asked. "Where have they taken my aunt?"

Robin explained what Mme Georges had done, while Jo chimed in with comments. Sylvie staggered back.

"You mean Aunt Amélie was *une voleuse,* a thief?" she asked. "She was not nice to me, but I never realized she was so bad."

"What will you do now?" Robin asked.

Sylvie glanced shyly at Marc, and then said, "I will go back to my studies. I wanted to be a teacher before Aunt Amélie made me stop and work for her."

"In fact, Sylvie did most of the work while her aunt lazed around," Marc said. "Then, when I finish school we will get married. Her aunt would not hear of it before. She wanted to keep Sylvie as her slave for life, but now she can not stand in our way." He clasped Sylvie's hand in his.

Sylvie blushed. "So that's why you turned red when I asked you if you told your aunt everything," Robin said, grinning.

The priest came up to the inspector, and chattered away to him in French, now and then glaring at Robin and Jo.

"What's he saying?" Robin asked Sylvie.

"He is saying that my aunt told him you were thieves, and that he almost had you arrested. The inspector is telling him the truth."

The priest looked shocked for a minute, then he patted Jo on the shoulder. "*La pauvre,*" he said, and shuffled off back to his duties.

"I hope this has not ruined Paris for you," Sylvie said earnestly.

"Of course not," said Robin. "We've had a really good time, despite everything."

"It's been fun," said Jo. "And I didn't have to eat anything creepy."

"Ah, but tonight we will make a feast for you to make up for my aunt's ill treatment of you," Sylvie said. "Inspector, you are invited. Nicolette will make the dishes that she is famous for."

"Nicolette," Robin said. "She warned us to be careful. Did she know anything about what your aunt was doing?"

"I am sure she did not," said Sylvie. "She tells everyone to be careful. She is like a mother to all the children who come to the house."

As the group began walking out of the cathedral, Jo turned to Marc and asked, "What dishes is Nicolette famous for?"

He grinned and then answered, "Apple tart. It is like a crisp apple pie."

"That sounds good," Jo said, licking her lips. "And what's the main course?"

Marc shook his head, and looked at Jo sympathetically. "Pig's feet."

Robin Bridge's Guide to Paris

Here are some sights in Paris that Jo and I saw. Remember, opening times, phone numbers, and addresses change sometimes, so you'll probably want to call ahead when you plan to visit these places.

① Bateaux-Mouches

As Marc had promised, we went on this boat tour of Paris at night. It was crowded and noisy, and it was hard to understand the taped narration in English because a lot of the listening devices were broken. We did see some beautiful sights, but this tour isn't as great as it could be. Maybe you'll have better luck with it.

Pont de l'Alma. ☎ 01-42-25-96-10. Daily, 10 a.m.–11:30 p.m. (May-October); 11 a.m.–9 p.m. (November-April). Admission fee.

② Berthillon

This has the most scrumptious ice cream in all Paris. It comes in all kinds of unusual flavors so Jo and I just pointed to the colors we liked best. I got a pink one that turned out to be some kind of berry and Jo got one that was crunchy with nuts and honey.

31 rue St-Louis-en-l'Ile. ☎ 01-43-54-31-61. Open 10 a.m.–8 p.m. Closed Monday, Tuesday, July, August, and Easter break.

③ The Bird Market

What a fun place! Jo and I could have spent hours here just looking at the birds. Some are absolutely beautiful with feathers all the colors of the rainbow. Sometimes the bird sellers will take the birds out of the cages and let them sit on your shoulders. If your parents are with you, they can shop while you look at the birds. There are a few shops behind the bird market that sell tablecloths, dried flowers, and other gifts.

Place Louis-Lépine on the Île de la Cité, no telephone, open on Sundays only. No admission fee.

④ Bois de Boulogne

This is the biggest park in Paris. It has the famous Roland-Garros stadium where the French Open tennis tournament is played every year. Unlike some of the other parks in Paris (see **Jardin du Luxembourg**), you can sit on the grass here. You can rent a bike or a boat or take a ferry to the islands on the lake. This is a nice place to go when you get tired of sightseeing and just want to hang out.

Take the métro to Sablons, Porte Maillot, Porte Dauphine, or Porte d'Auteuil. Open dawn to dusk. Go in daytime only. No admission fee.

⑤ Centre Georges Pompidou and Musée National D'art Moderne

The first time we saw this place we couldn't believe it was a museum. It looks like a building with its pipes hanging out. There are big, colored tubes all over it. The coolest thing is to go up the escalator inside. You ride up through one of the clear tubes and you can see outside. Inside, there isn't that much to see unless you're crazy about modern art. But outside, there's a whole sideshow going on with people juggling, eating fire, playing guitars, singing, and a lot more.

Place Georges Pompidou. ☎ 01-42-77-11-12. Open weekdays noon–10 p.m., weekends 10 a.m.–10 p.m. Closed Tuesdays. Admission fee, except Sunday is free.

⑥ La Conciergerie

Both of us loved this place. There are so many things to see. We liked Marie Antoinette's private chapel, with her initials in stained glass. When the French Revolution took place, the court issued 2,780 death proclamations from La Conciergerie. Upstairs, you can see the list of names of all those executed, and even a guillotine used on a murderer later on.

1 quai de l'Horloge. ☎ 01-43-54-30-06. Open daily April–September, 9:30 a.m.–6:30 p.m.; October–March, 10 a.m.–5 p.m. Admission fee.

⑦ Crypte Archéologique

If you're going to Notre Dame, stop here before or after, since it's right at the foot of the plaza. It's a little creepy with the dim lights, but kind of interesting to see parts of Paris from centuries ago. Jo and I loved the bits and pieces found when they started to dig. There was a little bronze spoon, a pewter baby's bottle from the 18th century, and a little bracelet that identified an orphan.

Place du Parvis Notre Dame. ☎ 01-43-29-83-51. Open daily April 1–September 30, 9:30 a.m.–6:30 p.m.; October 1–March 31, 10 a.m.– 5 p.m. Admission fee.

⑧ La Droguerie

This is a fun do-it-yourself jewelry place that Sylvie took us to one day. They've got tons of beads, ribbons, clasps—everything you could ever want to make your own necklaces and bracelets. Jo and I went wild here.

9 rue du Jour. ☎ 01-45-08-93-27. Call for hours open.

⑨ Les Égouts de Paris (The sewers of Paris)

Who would think a tour of Paris's sewers would be interesting, but Jo and I found this one of the best. It's dark and sometimes awfully smelly down there, but if you've read or seen Victor Hugo's *Les*

Miserables, you can imagine the hero, Jean Valjean, escaping through these wide tunnels. In some parts, you can actually see the water rushing through the tunnels.

Pont de l'Alma (at the corner of Quai D'Orsay and the Place de la Résistance). ☎ 01-53-68-27-81. Open Saturday–Wednesday: May 1–September 30, 11 a.m.–5 p.m.; October 1–April 30, 11 a.m.–4 p.m. Admission fee.

⑩ Tour Eiffel

There really is no place like the Eiffel Tower, whether you walk under it or go up to the top. We enjoyed going at night when the lights make it gleam. It's fun to walk the grounds and see people picnicking and enjoying the park. There really is graffiti on the railings. We couldn't believe it!

Champ de Mars. ☎ 01-44-11-23-23. Open daily 9 a.m.–11:30 p.m. (September–May); 9 a.m. –midnight (June–August). Admission fee.

⑪ Hôtel de Ville

The race was exciting to watch, but even if it's not the season for the race when you go, this building is fun to see because it's so decorated. The front has statues, roofs, doors, and all kinds of stuff on it. But if you walk behind it, the back of the building is very plain. This is Paris's city hall. There are tours but Jo and I didn't take one.

Place de l'Hôtel de Ville. ☎ 01-42-76-43-43. Official tour: Monday, 10:30 a.m. No admission fee.

⑫ Jardin du Luxembourg

Be careful here, and in many parks in Paris. If you accidentally walk on the grass (Jo did once), a policeman will scold you. Most of the time, you have to walk on a path covered with dirt and gravel. The best thing about this park is the puppet shows they have. They are really fun and reminded Jo and me of the one we saw in London in Covent Garden.

Enter at Place Edmond-Rostand. Like most parks in Paris, the Jardin du Luxembourg opens at 9 a.m. and closes at dusk. You will hear the park keeper's whistle when the gates are to be closed for the night. Puppet shows are at 3 and 4 p.m. on Wednesday, Saturday, and Sunday. Admission fee for puppet shows.

⑬ La Maison du Chocolat

The candy in Paris is amazing. I've never tasted anything so good. And it comes in such cute shapes. Once I saw a little chocolate porcupine with slivers of almonds for its quills. This place has super-premium chocolate. In the cold weather, it's known for its hot chocolate.

Three branches: 13a: 52 rue François 1er. ☎ 01-47-23-38-25; 13b: 8 blvd. de Madeleine, ☎ 01-47-42-86-52; 13c: 225 rue du Faubourg St.-Honoré, ☎ 01-42-27-39-44. All are open 9:30 a.m. –7 p.m. and closed Sundays. The one on rue de Faubourg is also closed on Mondays and the last week of July through the third week of August.

⑭ Marché aux Puces St-Ouen

There's lots to see and do here, but you have to like shopping. Jo was a little bored, but I loved it. We went back with Sylvie and I bought some advertising posters for my room at home and a very pretty bracelet. Don't accept the first price they give you. It's good to bargain here.

Take the métro to Porte de Clignancourt and when you get out, walk to the right. You can't miss it. The actual entrance to the flea market is near an underpass. Open Saturday, Sunday, and Monday. No admission fee.

⑮ Musée de Curiosité et de la Magie

Lots of fun even if it is a little corny. Jo loved it, and I think even older kids would find some of the exhibits interesting. Even though everything's in French, it's easy to understand.

11 rue Saint-Paul. ☎ 01-42-72-13-26. Open Friday, Saturday, and Sunday, 2 p.m.–7 p.m. Admission fee.

⑯ Musée des Parfumeries-Fragonard

Even though the main idea is to sell perfume here, this is such a cool place. We loved the exhibits of the perfume bottles, lipsticks, and other cosmetics. It was great to be able to sample all the perfume. The perfume comes in really pretty little gold bottles. There were tours but it seems they are only in French. Anyway, you don't really need one here.

9 rue Scribe. ☎ 01-47-42-93-40. Open Monday–Saturday, 9 a.m.–5:30 p.m. No admission fee.

⑰ Musée d'Orsay

Lots of paintings to see here. Jo wasn't so crazy about the museum, but she liked the big railroad clock. They have a nice café here, where you can eat outdoors or in. It's easy to get lost because the layout is a little confusing, but there are plenty of museum maps.

62 rue de Lille. ☎ 01-40-49-48-14. Open Tuesday–Saturday, 10 a.m.–6 p.m. (on Thursday open until 9:45 p.m.; from mid-June to mid-September opens at 9 a.m.); Sunday 9 a.m.–6 p.m. Admission fee.

⑱ Musée du Louvre

This place is huge! When we went with Mme Georges, we wouldn't have known where to go if she hadn't steered us around. Everything is divided in to *salles,* or rooms. If you want to go where we went, go to Salle 6 in the Denon Wing. There you'll see the huge painting *The Feast at Cana* that Jo and I stared at. Near the end of that room is the Mona Lisa. You'll be able to tell by the big crowd around it. Honestly, Jo and I didn't think it was that great. If you want to see a portrait like the one that was stolen from the *château,* go to Salle 77, right behind *The Feast at Cana.* Look for the portrait *Mademoiselle Caroline Rivière* by Jean-Auguste Ingres. When you leave, if you go through the carrousel area, you'll find shops where you can buy postcards and other souvenirs.

Entrance off place du Carrousel. ☎ 01-40-20-53-17. Open
Wednesday–Monday; Wednesday 9 a.m.–10 p.m., Thursday–Monday
9 a.m. –6 p.m.; Richelieu open Monday until 10 p.m. Admission fee.
First Sunday of each month free admission.

⑲ Notre-Dame

After all the excitement was over, Jo and I went back to the
cathedral. We climbed up one of the towers with Marc and Sylvie
who showed us a beautiful view of Paris. We also got to stare, up
close, at the hideous gargoyles that decorate the church. In *The
Hunchback of Notre Dame,* this is where Quasimodo rang the bells.

6 place du Parvis Notre Dame ☎ 01-42-34-56-10. Open daily 8 a.m.–
6:45 p.m. No admission fee. Towers are open daily 9:30 a.m.–6 p.m.
(April–September); 10 a.m.–4:15 p.m. October–March). ☎ 01-43-29-
50-40. Admission fee.

⑳ Place des Vosges

Marc told us that in 1605 King Henri IV tried to make this into a
royal residence, but he died before he could move in. The king's and
queen's palaces are the ones with the biggest fronts facing each other
across the park. Jousting took place in the middle area. This is a great
place to stop and rest and have a snack, particularly when it's hot
out.

In the Marais quarter, near the end of rue des Francs-Bourgeois. Open
daily. No admission fee.

㉑ La Samaritaine

Sylvie told us the food is not great here, so we just went for a snack.
The ice cream is good, but the view is the best. It's amazing. This is a
big department store with plenty of shopping.

Be sure to go to Building 2 where the rooftop café is. 19 rue de la
Monnaie. ☎ 01-40-41-20-20. Open Monday–Saturday from about
9:30 a.m.–7:00 p.m. No admission fee.

Robin Bridge's Paris Web Sites Review

Before we went to Paris, Jo and I tried to find some Web sites to look for some cool places. There were lots of sites for Disneyland, but not much for kids in Paris itself. We liked **www.timeout.com/paris** the best. They tell you about food and things to do and there's a neat money converter that shows you what the U.S. dollar is worth compared to the money in other countries. The shopping part was no good. All it told about was clothes for really little kids. We tried **www.about.com** and it sent us to **www.paris-touristoffice.com**. This was more of a grown-up site that told us about some of the things to see in Paris. A lot was for very young kids. Kids in Paris, part of the site, had a few cute things like how animals sound in different languages. Again, for very little kids. French Resources for Kids at **www.nhptv.org** was helpful if you need to use a dictionary or want to take a virtual tour of the Louvre or the Eiffel Tower. There was a site there for teens that looked interesting but it was all in French. For links to places we went to, go to **www.fourcornersbooks.com**. That Web site also has information on our trip to London and other cool trips you can take.

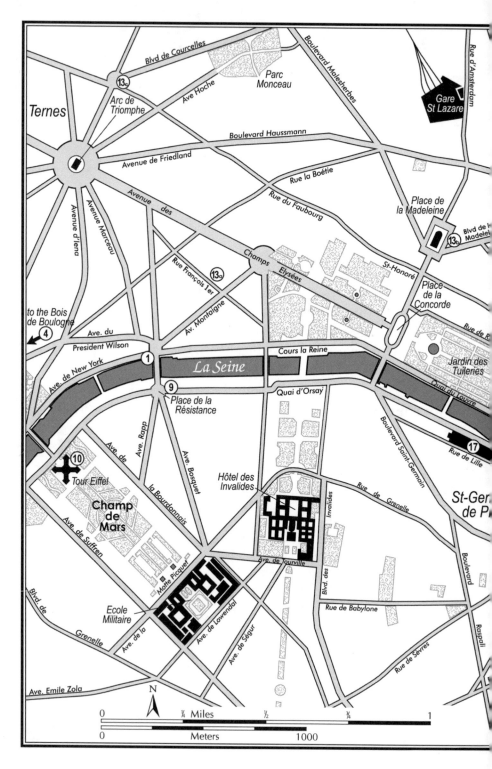

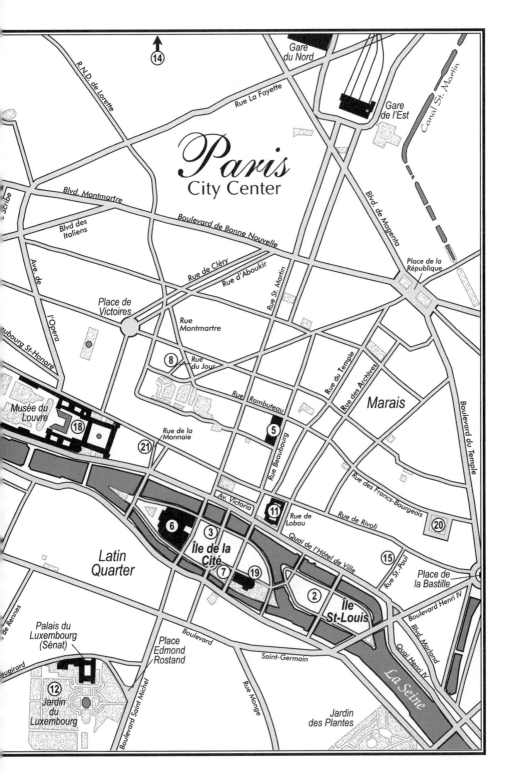

Paris
City Center

Gare du Nord

Gare de l'Est

Canal St. Martin

R.N.D. de Lorette

Rue La Fayette

Blvd. de Magenta

Place de la République

Blvd. Montmartre

Boulevard de Bonne Nouvelle

Blvd des Italiens

Rue de Cléry

Rue d'Aboukir

Rue St. Martin

Ave. de l'Opéra

Place de Victoires

Rue Montmartre

Rue du Temple

(8)

Rue du Jour

Rue des Archives

Rue Rambuteau

Marais

Musée du Louvre

(18)

Rue de la Monnaie

(5)

Rue Beaubourg

Boulevard du Temple

(21)

Av. Victoria

(11)

Rue de Lobau

Rue des Francs-Bourgeois

Rue de Rivoli

(20)

(6)

(3)

Île de la Cité

Quai de l'Hôtel de Ville

Latin Quarter

(7)

(19)

(15)

Rue St-Paul

Place de la Bastille

(2)

Île St-Louis

Boulevard Henri IV

de Rennes

Palais du Luxembourg (Sénat)

Place Edmond Rostand

Boulevard

Saint-Germain

Rue Monge

Blvd Morland

Quai Henri IV

ugirard

(12)

Jardin du Luxembourg

Boulevard Saint Michel

Jardin des Plantes

La Seine

Scribe

ubourg St-Honoré

This image of a monarch butterfly was chosen as a symbol
for the Going To series because monarchs are strong flyers geared
for travel. They migrate between warmer and cooler climates,
often ranging over several thousand miles in a single trip.